A tabby sauntered across the floor and vaulted onto the window ledge. It peered out the window as if searching for prey. A few feet away, Sergeant Hunt stood at the ticket counter, talking with the station clerk. He resembled the cat. Intent and focused. And quite handsome. Was he married? If not, then a bevy of unattached ladies at Fort Dent would surely vie for his attention. He would be a striking feather in some girl's cap. Not that she was looking for a feather. After all that had happened, her cap would remain unadorned for quite a while.

The sergeant nodded, took a slip of paper, and wheeled around. His benign expression revealed nothing of his negotiations. Had he been successful in securing passage for Orion? He certainly commanded respect with those golden eyes and deep, drilling voice. His demeanor exuded confidence and conviction. He was the type of man her father would expect her to marry. A soldier just like him. She wouldn't give him that satisfaction.

Magic
on His Mind

by

Donna Dalton

The Gifted, Book 3

Magic on His Mind

Cover Art by *Rae Monet, Inc. Design*

The Wild Rose Press, Inc.
PO Box 708
Adams Basin, NY 14410-0708
Visit us at www.thewildrosepress.com

Publishing History
First Edition, 2021
Trade Paperback ISBN 978-1-5092-3505-6
Digital ISBN 978-1-5092-3506-3

The Gifted, Book 3
Published in the United States of America

I dedicate this book
to my mother Margaret Alley
and her sister Ellen Simpson
for whom the main character is named.
Their love and support means the world to me,
and I take inspiration from their joy of life and family.

Chapter One

Meadowdale Farms
Northern Virginia
May 1889

Warmth swirled in his skull. His scalp tingled. His temples pulsed. Circles were simple. A line with no beginning and no end. Other shapes, like stars, were not as easy to form and keep afloat. Those required a little more effort.

Gabe gave a mental push. The porcelain lady exited the ring of gee-gaws hovering over the table. Then the little silver bell left. Then the marble balls. He prodded again. The floaters danced and jiggled. Another push and the objects formed the shape of a five-pointed star with the dinner bell dinging softly at the apex. Spectacular, his sister would say. To him, just a way to pass the time.

Speaking of time…he glanced at the mantel clock. Quarter after ten. Where the hell was everyone? The Wheaton's butler had abandoned him in this parlor from Hades nearly an hour ago. Heavy purple curtains blockaded the sunlight. The room smelled of beeswax and old ashes. Bulky, claw-footed furnishings crowded the floor, and the banked hearth fire spewed tidal waves of heat. His uniform would soon become sweat-logged and reeking. Wouldn't that make for a great first impression.

Another mental thrust sent the menagerie spinning counterclockwise. Mrs. Campbell, the matron of Seaton House orphanage, would be proud of his accomplishments. She had rescued him from an abusive guardian hell-bent on beating his impulsiveness out of him…a useless endeavor since his urges had a mind of their own. Yet, with Mrs. Campbell's help and support, he had learned to tame his compulsions. And his gift. He'd started moving small, lifeless objects with his mind at age four. People and animals were immune to his talent. Probably a good thing.

The clack of footfalls came from the hallway. *Cripes.* Someone was coming and coming at a quick clip. Only a few people outside the orphanage knew about his gift. Being abnormal didn't sit well with most folks, and what he needed to do required appearing ordinary as a pebble on a sandy beach.

He pulled back, shutting off the flow of energy spewing from his skull. The hovering items drifted down and settled on the table. Motionless and clustered just as they had been arranged, or as close as he could remember.

"Good morning, Sergeant Hunt," a woman said as she sailed into the room, toting a serving tray. "I am Mrs. Wheaton. I apologize for keeping you waiting. I had to see to a matter in the kitchen. Reliable help is *so* difficult to come by these days."

He pried his rear from the grip of the over-stuffed chair and stood. No more tomfoolery. If Mrs. Wheaton had caught sight of those floating objects, she might very well reconsider allowing her niece to travel with him. That couldn't happen. His future in the army depended on the successful completion of this mission. General Myer had made that fact quite clear.

"Not a problem, ma'am. It gave me time to review the schedule for our upcoming trip. I want this journey to go as smoothly as possible."

Mrs. Wheaton bent and set the tray on the table. Gray sliced her temples and speckled her eyebrows. Even her dark dress shimmered with silvery streaks. She rivaled the Seaton House freckled hens for vividness.

"As do I, Sergeant. As do I…" A frown creased her milky brow, and she reached to shift the porcelain lady back to what was most likely its preferred location. Her condemning gaze lifted and landed on him. She was as sharp-eyed as those speckled hens. He would do well to guard his words *and* his actions, else he risked a pecking.

"Margaret's traveling companion seems to be running late," she said. "While we wait for Mrs. Sommers to arrive, we can have tea and sweet biscuits."

"Thank you, ma'am. That sounds wonderful." He preferred coffee or even a stiff drink, but since travel arrangements and a cantankerous wagon mule had caused him to miss the morning meal, any refreshment would be welcome.

"Please resume your seat, Sergeant."

As he sat, she grasped the pitcher handle and began pouring tea into china cups decorated with vines of wandering roses. Delicate. And expensive. And requiring a gentle hand.

"Sugar? Milk?"

"Neither, thank you." The darker the better.

She handed him a steaming cup nestled on a saucer

and then set a plate of biscuits on the table in front of him. "How long you have been assigned to Fort Dent, Sergeant?"

He balanced the saucer on his knee just as Mrs. Campbell had taught. He would be the John D. Rockefeller of refinement. "I moved to the Oklahoma Territories when I was a small boy. Once old enough, I enlisted in the army and was lucky enough to be assigned to General Myer's command at Fort Dent."

"You are familiar with the area then."

More of a statement than a question. He popped a biscuit into his mouth and chewed while she settled on the settee across from him, fluffing skirts and pillows, and reminding him of a hen roosting on a laying box. He choked off a laugh with a gulp of tea.

"My brother has an annoying habit of sugar-coating life at the fort in his letters," she continued. "No outpost in the middle of Indian lands could be that marvelous. I suppose he thinks he's protecting my sensibilities, but I need the truth, the unvarnished truth."

"What is it you wish to know, ma'am?"

"Is this Fort Dent secure enough? Are the Indians contained? What would people think of me if I allowed my niece to travel to some dangerous place and she became hurt or worse."

"I assure you, Miss Myer will be quite safe. Fort Dent is the most secure outpost in the territories. Ten-foot stockade walls of thick, hewn logs and well-guarded parapets protect the enclosure. Though such defenses aren't as necessary as they used to be since the Indians have been relegated to reservations and seem content to stay there." For the most part. The recent

Ghost Dance rituals had frayed some nerves, but that outbreak seemed to have quieted.

She didn't look convinced. Dappled brows formed a thin line of disbelief.

"You have nothing to worry about, ma'am," he added. "Your niece will be well-protected, inside and outside the fort. Her father will see to that." General Edward Myer ran his outpost with an iron fist...one he wielded swiftly and without discrimination to ensure order and safety. Ten days in a disciplinary barrack cell for misconduct had taught him that lesson.

"My niece has lived here with us for most of her life, ever since her poor mother died, God rest her soul, and Edward left her in our care. Margaret is accustomed to the security and comfort of a genteel life."

Comforts indeed. Little Miss Silver Spoon wouldn't last a day in the backwoods. But that was General Myer's cross to bear. He just had to get her there.

"Pardon me, Madame," came a deep voice from the doorway. "Mrs. Sommers has arrived."

"Wonderful. Thank you, James. See her in."

The butler stepped aside, and a woman garbed in black waddled into the parlor. Dimples dug into plump, rosy cheeks. She had thick arms and a large girth, perfect for ache-soothing hugs, just like the ones Mrs. Clement, the housekeeper at Seaton House, gave.

"I apologize for my tardiness, Alma. I misplaced my spectacles, and it took forever to find them." The woman pushed wire-rimmed eyeglasses further up on her nose. "I can't see a thing without them, don't you know."

Mrs. Wheaton set her cup and saucer on the table.

"It's quite all right, Beatrice. We were just having tea while we waited. Please, come and join us."

The butler vanished just as quickly and quietly as he had appeared. If only he had such an asset on his scouting squad. Someone who could slip in and out of an enemy camp without notice. Like a ghost. His platoon would get all the plum assignments.

"Sergeant Hunt?"

Pale eyes widened by glass lenses blinked at him in expectation. *Cripes.* Caught woolgathering during introductions. He shoved the cup and saucer onto the table and pushed to his feet. "My apologies. It's a pleasure to meet you, ma'am. I look forward to traveling with you and Miss Myer."

The owlish gaze rolled around the room. "Where *is* Meggie? I expected everyone to be ready to leave the moment I arrived."

So did he. He stepped around the table. "Mrs. Sommers is right. We need to be on our way. Thank you for the refreshments, Mrs. Wheaton. If you'll excuse me, I'll go and make sure everything is ready for our trip. Please have everyone come out as soon as possible."

He threaded around the furniture and moved into the hallway. The astute butler met him at the front entrance, door open, and a U.S. Army slouch hat in hand. He thanked the man, took his hat, and plowed onto the veranda. Fresh air cooled his face and tamed the fire burning in his lungs. Perfect. Now he could breathe.

"Is everyone ready to leave, Sergeant?"

Private Dunn sat on the wagon seat, patiently holding the reins. Wrinkles cragged his sun-burnished face. His beard was more gray than brown. Dunn had joined the army before many of his fellow troopers had been born. He'd been Gabe's first choice for this mission. The older, wiser man kept to himself and didn't ask prying questions.

He tucked his hat on his head. "Just about. As you probably saw, the traveling companion has arrived. We're waiting on Miss Myer to come down, which should be soon." He hoped. If this tardiness became a habit, their schedule would turn to crap.

Something brushed his arm, and he turned. Raven eyes flashed up at him. Equally dark hair curled around a smooth, milk-white face. The young woman swiped a tongue over pouty lips. "My, my. You must be the escort."

He'd seen soiled doves with less invitation in their demeanor. He tipped a finger to his hat. "Sergeant Hunt, Miss Myer."

Her throaty laugh scraped at his ears. "La, don't you wish. I'm her cousin, Christina Wheaton."

That was a relief. He'd have a devil of a time keeping this one in line. Men would trail after her like stags in rut. A headache to be certain. "Pleased to meet you, Miss Wheaton. Is your cousin coming down? We need to be on our way."

Half-masted eyelids fluttered. "Is she not out here? She left her bedroom nearly an hour ago."

What the hell? Rumor at the fort said General Myer and his daughter had a strained relationship. Had she cut and run to avoid going to live with him?

A commotion sounded and then a horse and rider rounded the side of the house. Long legs and nicely sloped hips accented the stallion's near-perfect conformation. Its black satin coat glistened like polished glass. But the dainty lady perched on the animal's back grabbed the attention.

She sat easily in the sidesaddle, gloved hands light on the reins. Blonde ringlets bounced around a pretty, oval face. A pale purple riding outfit hugged slender curves. Feminine perfection. And way above his station.

"That, my dear Sergeant Hunt," came a sugary drawl near his ear. "Is my cousin, Margaret Ellen Myer. Meg to her friends and family. She's quite the equestrian, wouldn't you say?"

Quite. But they didn't have time for a pleasure ride...of any sort. "Pardon me, Miss Wheaton. I need to speak with your cousin."

As he started for the steps, a hand on his arm stopped him. "Don't go falling under Meg's spell, Sergeant. Miss Perfect is anything but. Guard your heart around her."

Good grief. With family like the Wheatons, who needed enemies? "Fear not," he replied. "I have no interest in Miss Myer or her affairs."

He extracted his arm and descended the steps. At the bottom, he met horse and rider. Eyes blue as a summer sky rolled over him. Not in a saucy way like her cousin. More like a queen eyeballing a peasant.

He swept off his hat and dipped a nod. "Good morning, Miss Myer. I'm Sergeant Hunt, your escort for the trip. Please allow me to help you dismount and board Mrs. Sommers's buggy. We need to leave now else we risk missing our train."

"There's no need for that, Sergeant. I will be riding Orion to the train station."

Perhaps she suffered with travel sickness and preferred to ride horseback rather than in the jostling buggy. Several of the orphans at Seaton House contended with such an affliction. "Very well. You can leave the horse at the livery in town and have someone from Meadowdale fetch him later."

"Oh, no. Orion is coming with me."

"Pardon?"

"I'm taking him with me to Fort Dent."

Oh, *hell* no. "I'm sorry, but that is out of the question. I've already made all the arrangements for our trip. No provisions have been made for a horse."

"Then you will have to make some."

"Your father only provided funds for the passage of four people. There's not enough to cover a horse."

"I have my own money. I will pay for his passage."

Irritation rose inside him. He swallowed back a curse. "We're running behind schedule as it is. We won't have time to gather the things a horse will need...not to mention finding space for him on the train."

"We will wait for another train then."

Lord save him from obstinate women. "The next train to Chicago won't leave until tomorrow. Delaying our departure will disrupt all the arrangements that have been made for the entire trip. It's just not feasible to do that for a horse."

"Orion is not just any horse."

He reached up and patted a silky muzzle. The animal gave him a gentle nudge. Based on its owner's behavior, he half expected bared teeth or a nip. "Be that as it may, your request is unrealistic. We have to stick to our planned schedule."

"If Orion doesn't go, I don't go."

That shoved-up chin and thinned lips spoke volumes. His sister Sally often looked the same when digging in her heels.

It appeared his mission was going to be anything *but* smooth.

****

The Sterling stationhouse smelled of freshly lumbered wood and paint. Cheery gingham curtains decorated the windows. A coat of whitewash brightened the walls, and a black potbelly stove oozed warmth from the corner. The new owners had made many improvements since the last time she'd been inside. Two years ago, Aunt Alma had allowed her to join the expedition to Washington City to purchase material for Christina's debutante gown. Since she was also of age, she had been permitted to select a bolt. Not as luxurious as Christina's satin, but at least it hadn't been a hand-me-down.

A thin layer of padding on the bench made waiting on the train much easier on the backside. Unfortunately, it did little to cushion her worries. Thoughts of the trip ahead bashed in her head like waves in a nor'easter. She shifted and rolled the stiffness out of her shoulders. Everything would turn out just fine. It had to. She couldn't go west without Orion. The stallion was a reminder of everything safe and secure in her life. If he wasn't there to be her anchor, she would drown.

Her aunt and uncle were not happy with her decision to take Orion. They had never warmed to the notion of a lady handling a stallion. A mare or gelding, yes, but a stud horse…it just wasn't done. But they had finally relented. Perhaps they felt pity for her situation.

Or perhaps they just wanted her gone.

Her stomach churned around the breakfast biscuit she'd managed to choke down. Was she doing the right thing? Tucking tail and running seemed to be the coward's way out. She should stay and accept the consequences of her actions. Yet if she did, the Wheatons would continue to be painted with the same tarnished brush. They didn't deserve to be maligned because of her folly.

Aunt Alma and Uncle Robert had taken her in when her mother died. They had fed and clothed her. Had provided her with a robust education. Had even treated her with their own brand of benevolence. She would miss them. But while Meadowdale Farms would always hold a special place in her heart, she never felt a deep connection to it. Never felt as if she truly belonged. Maybe one day, she would find such a place.

A tabby sauntered across the floor and vaulted onto the window ledge. It peered out the window as if searching for prey. A few feet away, Sergeant Hunt stood at the ticket counter, talking with the station clerk. He resembled the cat. Intent and focused. And quite handsome. Was he married? If not, then a bevy of unattached ladies at Fort Dent would surely vie for his attention. He would be a striking feather in some girl's cap. Not that she was looking for a feather. After all that had happened, her cap would remain unadorned for quite a while.

The sergeant nodded, took a slip of paper, and wheeled around. His benign expression revealed nothing of his negotiations. Had he been successful in securing passage for Orion? He certainly commanded respect with those golden eyes and deep, drilling voice.

His demeanor exuded confidence and conviction. He was the type of man her father would expect her to marry. A soldier just like him. She wouldn't give him that satisfaction.

"Well, Sergeant Hunt?"

He stopped in front of her, uniform hat in hand. Sunlight spewed through the window and burnished his short-cropped, sand-colored hair in a golden halo. Even his smooth-shaven face glowed with vitality. All she felt was darkness.

"It appears we have not missed our train after all," he said. "It was delayed in Washington City and will be here within the hour."

"And Orion?"

The skin over his jaw twitched as if he chewed on something tough. "I was able to secure passage for your horse."

"There, you see. It all worked out."

He merely stared down at her, those leonine eyes prowling over her. She squirmed on the bench seat but refused to break eye contact. If he thought he had the upper hand, she would become easy prey. She was tired of being a victim. Bone tired.

He gave a grunt that could have meant anything and snuggled his uniform hat on his head. "I'm going over to the supply store across the street and see about getting some grain and hay delivered for the trip."

She pushed upright. "I'll come with you. I want to purchase a bag of apples. Orion has a sweet tooth. A very *long* sweet tooth."

"I can get the apples while I'm there if you'd like. Save you the trouble."

"It's no trouble. We'll be sitting at length once we

board the train. I want to stretch my legs before that happens. Mrs. Sommers can watch over our things until we return."

A soft snore rumbled from the woman sitting on the bench, eyes closed, and chin almost touching her chest. Wire-rimmed spectacles teetered on the edge of a pudgy nose, ready to fall at the least jostle. Maybe *watch* wasn't quite the appropriate word.

The sergeant made a noise that sounded halfway between a laugh and a cough. "Yes, well, Private Dunn should be back soon from delivering the rented wagon to the livery and watering Orion. He will look after your things…and Mrs. Sommers."

Was that laughter sparking those golden eyes? Maybe the sergeant wasn't as starchy as he made out to be. What kind of man was he? He must be trustworthy, else her father would never have assigned him the task of escorting her across the country. No matter how much he detested her, the principled Edward Myer would not stint on his daughter's protection.

"Miss Myer, are you coming? We only have a half hour at most to complete our errand."

His challenge poked into her gloom. She gathered a handful of skirt and aimed for the door. She would not let thoughts of her father pull her down. She would be the strong, capable lady Sam had always admired.

Sam. A block down from the train station, he had coaxed a mongrel from under the boardwalk and nurtured the starving pup back to life. He had repaired the rotted planks in front of Mrs. Treadwell's house so the elderly widow wouldn't trip and fall. The crippled milliner's display window had never sparkled so brightly. Sam was the kindest man she had ever known.

He was the brother she never had. He knew everything about her as she did about him. A pang stabbed her heart. Where was he now? How was he faring? It had been nearly two months since they last spoke.

She sighed and rubbed the string circling her right index finger. It was yellow. Sam's favorite. He said the color made him think of happy, sunny days. She wore the string as a reminder of him, of what he meant to her, and of what she had done to him. However unintentional, his dismissal from the farm had been her fault.

"Is everything all right, Miss Myer? You look troubled."

She shook off her sadness and stepped off the boardwalk and onto the cobbled street. Sam had urged her to move on with her life. To find happiness. She would do her best to follow his advice.

"I'm fine," she said. "Just concerned about Orion and how he will handle the trip. He's not a young colt anymore."

The sergeant fell into step beside her. "He looks to be in fine health. Your horse shouldn't have any issues."

Orion wasn't the only one who appeared to be in fine health. Sergeant Hunt's dark blue uniform hugged a lean, agile form. A yellow stripe running down the outside of each trouser leg accented long, nimble limbs. She had to double-step to keep up.

"I didn't catch your given name, Sergeant."

"It's Gabe. Gabriel Michael."

"Ah, the archangels."

"My parents had a sense of humor, it seems."

"Are you not an angel then?"

His face tightened, lips thinning into a firm line. There was more to him than greeted the eye. A lot more. Oddly, she wanted to learn all about him. Where he came from. What he liked. What he disliked. Sam had often warned her that curiosity killed cats.

He held out a hand to help her onto the boardwalk on the other side of the street. She gave his fingers the briefest touch. It would be best to keep her relationship with Sergeant Hunt on an impersonal level. Any more blows and her heart would shatter into a million pieces.

He bounded onto the porch and crossed to push open the door. An overhead bell dinged softly, announcing their arrival. She sailed past him and into the store. The smell of oldness greeted her. Old wood and old iron. Sterling Mercantile had been the cornerstone of the town that formed along the railroad tracks almost a century ago. It had seen the town grow from a few buildings to dozens in an effort to attract residents from Washington City who might want to escape the city for a weekend or to enjoy a peaceful summer retreat.

"I see an apple barrel over by that far window," Sergeant Hunt said. "You gather a bagful and meet me at the counter. I'll speak with the clerk about feed and hay. Our errand should go faster that way."

She nodded and angled across the store to a large wooden barrel sitting under a window. The perfume of freshly harvested fruit assailed her. Memories surfaced of her and Sam sitting on a stout branch, enjoying a late afternoon snack. There was nothing tastier than an apple plucked fresh off the tree.

She picked up a burlap bag from a nearby stack and shook it open. Using her free hand, she selected an apple and gently squeezed. It was firm with no bruising or pits. She brought it to her nose and drew in the aroma. Fruity and sweet. Perfect. She slipped the apple into the bag. Only the finest specimens for Orion.

A movement outside the window drew her attention. Nearly a dozen children of various sizes spewed from the schoolhouse door and swarmed into the yard, yelling and cavorting at their freedom. She and Christina had not been allowed to attend the town school. Instead, Aunt Alma had secured tutors for them. The only outside instruction they received had been from the pastor at Saint Michael's Episcopal Church.

Located at the far end of the street, the church wasn't visible from the mercantile window. But the tall spires and carved granite walls were clear as glass in her mind. As were the condemning stares and whispered comments thrown at her as she trailed the Wheatons to their pew. Unkindness, it appeared, knew no boundaries, even in a house of God.

She turned her attention back to the apples and soon had a bag bulging with fruit. She secured the opening with twine and joined Sergeant Hunt at the counter. He took the bag from her and pushed coins across the countertop. Before leaving Meadowdale Farms, she had handed over the funds for Orion's care. Etiquette required a man to handle such things. While she bucked at the restriction, she would comply. If she ever had a chance to come back, perhaps her conformity would make her return smoother.

Sergeant Hunt strode to the door and held it open for her. A satisfied smile dimpled his cheeks. "That went well. Grain and hay are already on the way over to the stationhouse."

She pointed to the bag he held. "And the apples are fresh and firm. Orion should be quite content, despite the cramped traveling conditions."

As she stepped out onto the boardwalk, a stiff gust plowed down the street. Grit stung her face, and her bonnet shifted. She turned against the wind and into the path of two approaching ladies, one older, the other younger. Narrowed green eyes glared from beneath a lace-trimmed hat brim while pale lips thinned into a long, disapproving line. She knew that look. Knew it well. It was all she had seen over the past two months.

She dipped a nod. "Good afternoon, Mrs. Ellsworth. Miss Daniella."

The woman snagged her daughter's hand and scurried past, her pointy nose aimed skyward. Heat blossomed in Meg's neck and rose into her ears. There would be more cuts like that in a town where everyone knew everyone else's affairs. Her smooth return would have a long wait.

Gentle fingers closed around her arm. "What was that about?"

"It was nothing. We should return to the stationhouse. The train will be arriving soon." The sooner, the better. It was time to put Sterling and all its ugliness behind her.

"It was not nothing. Those women were rude. What do they hold against you?"

"It is none of your concern."

"General Myer placed me in charge of your care. If anything has happened that impinges on that duty, it becomes my concern."

A dark cloud overran the sun, plunging the street into darkness. Teddy's expression had turned that exact same shade of gray…stormy and full of wrath. It seemed like only yesterday when he had sauntered into the barn and found her in Sam's arms, platonic though the gesture had been. He had dismissed her explanation without a second thought. Had condemned her and called her horrid names. He had retracted his offer of marriage and left, never to be seen again. The injustice of his reaction still stung. If he loved her half as much as he professed, he should have trusted her.

She blinked away a rising film of tears and gathered her skirts. "We should go. I thought I heard a train whistle."

The last thing she wanted was to explain the true reason for her trip west. She already held enough contempt for herself to fill an ocean.

Chapter Two

Dying sunlight painted the motionless railcars a dull, orange hue. The train had stopped to take on fuel and to allow the passengers to have dinner at the trackside inn. A simple fare, but enjoyable. His grumbling belly had thanked him. But now that the layover was nearing an end, he had to get his charges back on board.

Weedy grass slapped at his boots as he walked. Overhead, a flock of blackbirds dipped and soared, enjoying one last frolic before roosting for the night. It had been a long, tiresome day. He looked forward to settling down as well, though the hard, second-class coach bench would offer little in sleeping comfort.

Per his commander's instructions, he had secured Miss Myer and Mrs. Sommers a berth in a Pullman car. Padded chairs, carpeted floors, and pull-down sleeping cots with feather mattresses would see the ladies through the trip in comfort and luxury. He and Private Dunn would make do with coach class. They had endured worse conditions while out on patrol and survived.

Beyond the caboose, a black horse grazed in a patch of grass growing near the tracks. A purple hat feather peeked over the stallion's back. A most intriguing feather. It was long and thick, and the tip curled over like the tail on a squirrel. It had bobbed as

Miss Myer pecked at her meal and nodded in response to Mrs. Sommers's ceaseless chatter. Up and down, tagging an eyebrow and then an earlobe. The thing was more suited to a bedroom than a dinner table. Rosita had enjoyed his skillful tickles and implored him to bring a feather whenever he visited Miss Ruby's Club for Gentlemen. After this mission, he might just have to pay the establishment a visit.

Miss Myer had excused herself from the dinner table and took her feathery temptation with her. A good thing. He had a difficult enough time controlling his compulsiveness as it was. No need to prod it with lustful thoughts that could *never* be acted on. If he did, he would find himself tied to the nearest gallows. General Myer would not have his daughter's reputation tarnished, especially by a troublemaker who didn't have a hair of a chance of making a list of prospective husbands.

"I'm so sorry to put you through all this distress," came a soft murmur from the other side of the stallion.

He pulled up short. What the hell? Was she a mind reader like Anna at the orphanage? While the gifted were few and far between, there were still pockets of them that remained undiscovered.

"Taking you away from your animal friends. Making you stand in that stuffy old horse car for hours on end. As much as I hate doing that to you, I couldn't leave Meadowdale without you."

He pushed out a breath of relief. She was only talking to the horse who appeared to have little interest in her apology. The animal merely nosed deeper into the grass, raking the spindly blades with its teeth.

"I will make it up to you, I promise. Once we reach

Fort Dent, you will be treated to the grand life you deserve. All the other horses will be green with envy."

Gabe grunted under his breath. Whatever she expected at Dent, it wouldn't be grand. Most of the buildings were made of thin planks that let in the summer heat and barely blocked the chills of winter. In the dry months, the air was so clogged with dirt, breathing became a chore. And the flies. Lord help the creature, animal or human, who got stuck in a horde of those relentless pests. Welts from their bites itched for days.

"I don't know what I would do without you, Orion. You have been my rock. My savior. You have helped me through more bad days than I can count. Where we are going, I will need your love and loyalty more than ever. I h-hope you understand."

Her soft sob shuffled across the short distance. His heart stuttered. He wanted to take her in his arms. Comfort her. But he couldn't. For so very many reasons. Best to just think of her as a duty; one to be carried out with honor and integrity.

He aimed for the cinder-strewn path running along the rails. Hopefully, the crunch of his footfalls would provide enough noise to announce his presence without startling the pair. He didn't want the horse to bolt and cause Miss Myer to get hurt.

His boot heel rasped on a cluster of rocks. The stallion snorted and jerked up his head. Brown eyes glared in his direction, but the animal remained rooted in place. Fine horse, that one.

A hat-bedecked head peeked from beneath the stallion's neck. "Is someone there?"

He waved a hand. "It's just me, Miss Myer. We

need to get Orion loaded back onto the train. Our supper layover is nearly at an end."

She ducked behind her four-legged barricade. "Oh. I…um…j-just give me a minute, please."

Her voice was husky and thick. Why had she been crying? He should offer the use of his handkerchief, but that would expose his eavesdropping. He didn't have enough fingers and toes to count the times his ears had been boxed after getting caught listening in on private conversations.

He stopped on the other side of the horse and gave the animal a gentle pat. Orion snorted again, softer this time, and then nosed back into the grass, apparently no longer seeing him as a threat.

"When I didn't find you in your railcar," he said, "I figured you had come out to visit with Orion. He appears to be tolerating the train ride without any issues."

"Yes. H-he's handling the trip quite well."

"How about you, Miss Myer? You left the dinner table rather abruptly. Are you suffering from travel sickness?"

A long inhale rode the air. A few seconds later, the shuffle of skirts sounded and then, Miss Myer emerged in front of the horse, one hand fisting a balled-up white hankie. Redness tipped her nose and ringed her eyes. A smear of wet streaked her cheek. Was she upset about leaving her home and the only family she had ever known? Or was it someone more personal she had left behind? Someone who held her heart.

"Thank you for your concern, Sergeant, but I'm fine." She averted her gaze and combed gloved fingers through a black mane. "As you surmised, I just wanted to see Orion before our journey resumed. Make sure he is well fed and comfortable before bedding down for the night."

"There's no need to worry over Orion. I paid the attendant extra coins to make sure your horse gets all he needs."

Her mouth tipped into a wry smile. He wanted to trace those pink lips with a finger. Feel their smoothness. Taste them with his tongue. He fisted his saber handle instead.

"I know he's getting the best possible care," she said. "But I had to make certain. I wanted him to see a familiar face. Let him know he wasn't forgotten."

"It's clear how much you care for him."

"He's very special to me…has been ever since he was born." She tugged on the lead rope. "Come on, boy. It's time to go."

The horse left his dinner without complaint and started forward. Gabe fell into step beside them. He focused on the path ahead and not on the wicked hat feather stroking the top of a pink ear.

"You seem quite comfortable around Orion. Most ladies in my experience wouldn't come near a stallion of his size."

"I trust Orion. Always have. He's like a son to me. When his mother's milk failed to come in and his health began to fail, they talked of putting him down. I couldn't allow that, so I convinced Uncle Robert to let me take over his care. Every two hours I fed him fresh cow's milk from a bottle. He drank every drop and looked for more." Her tone lightened. "You'd think he'd been born a piglet."

He tossed a sideways glance at her. The sadness

weighing her face had lifted. Her eyes were bright and clear. Good. A happy general's daughter meant a happy general.

"I once helped my sister with a litter of orphaned kittens. Coyotes had killed the mother. Caring for those little fur-bundles was an endless chore, but Sally didn't give up. Every one of them survived."

"Your sister sounds like a girl after my own heart. Does she live near you at Fort Dent?"

"Sally lives in Mineral. That's the town just outside the fort. Once you get settled, if you're of a mind to venture out, try the Lacy Lady. It's a restaurant near the train station. My sister and some of our friends from Seaton House run the place."

"Seaton House?"

"It's a home for orphaned children. After our parents died, my sister and I lived there until we were old enough to be out on our own." There was more to the loss of their mother and father and going to live at Seaton House. A lot more. But he didn't want to bring her down with such a gloomy tale.

"I'm sorry to hear about your parents. I too lost my mother at a young age." Her steps slowed, and her voice turned pensive. "Were you treated well at this orphanage? I've read accounts of abuse committed at some homes."

"Not at Seaton House. We were all treated with compassion and fairness. The matron, Mrs. Campbell, was stern when she had to be, loving when not. She was like a mother to us." And more. Seaton House was no ordinary orphanage. All the children living there had special talents...talents that, if discovered, could get them banished from society, or worse. Mrs. Campbell taught them how to fit in by concealing their gifts and using them only when necessary.

"She sounds wonderful. You're lucky to have found a place with caring people."

Sadness tinted her tone. Had she not been happy at Meadowdale Farms? The Wheatons appeared to be caring people…well, except for the raven-eyed Christina. Did jealousy have a hand in the girl's malicious behavior? He'd once felt the stab of someone's envy. After inviting him to join their "boys' club," Pete Cavendish had become resentful over his quick rise in favor. He'd convinced the other boys of his oddness, and they'd turned on him. They had left him bruised and bleeding in a puddle of mud. That's where Lieutenant Preston Booth had found him and where his desire to join the army had taken root. As Mrs. Campbell often said, *silver linings form on all types of clouds*.

"I am indeed fortunate," he said. "Everyone at Seaton House became my family. They still are." A thought surfaced, and eagerness rose inside him. "I have an idea. Why don't you join Sally and me on one of our visits to the orphanage? You can meet Mrs. Campbell and the others living there."

"I'd like that very much."

So would he. It would give him an excuse to see Miss Myer again. It would also give her an opportunity to see where he had come from. Meet the people he loved and respected.

The ramp leading into the horse car loomed ahead. The red-haired attendant stood at the opening, watching their approach. A good man, Ned. Irishman. Excellent with horses. And people. He'd put Miss Myer at ease with kind words and a gentle demeanor.

Gabe reached for the rope. "I'll lead Orion up to Ned if you'd like. That ramp is rather steep."

A smile that would chase clouds from the sun stretched across her face. "That's not necessary. Orion can do it on his own."

She draped the rope across the stallion's back and pointed to the opening. "Up you go, Orion."

The stallion clattered up the ramp and dove into the horse car without an ounce of hesitation. The officers in his cavalry unit would chomp at the bit to own such a marvelous animal. "That's one well-trained horse."

"He likes to please me, so his training has been easy. He doesn't give me any trouble."

"I have to admit, I expected him to cause a ruckus at being confined for such a long period of time. Stallions can be temperamental creatures. I'm grateful he has proven me wrong."

She rested a hand on his arm and turned that sunny smile on him. "And I'm grateful for all you have done for him. Your efforts on his behalf are much appreciated."

Heat from her fingertips seared his skin through the wool sleeve. Desire trotted through him. *He* wanted to please her…in many fascinating ways, starting with that hat feather. He'd work his way across her cheek and down her neck. Loosen the buttons on her blouse and delve into—

A warning toot blasted into his wayward thoughts. He cleared his throat and nodded at the railcars. "That's the signal to board. We should be going."

She removed her hand and angled for the front of the train. Her backside swayed in seductive wiggles. He didn't want to be attracted to her. Didn't want to like her. She was a duty, a step on his ladder to a rise in rank. But dang if she hadn't snuggled against his chest like a kitten with a tummy full of milk.

****

Even with the windows closed, the clickety-clack of iron wheels droned inside the railcar. It was monotonous and irksome, the sound ticking off the miles lengthening between her and everything familiar and safe.

Meadowdale had been her home for as far back as she could remember. The main house had nourished and cradled her. In later years, the barns became a refuge and the rolling pastures her escape paths. Would she find Fort Dent as accommodating? What of the man who had summoned her there? Why had he sent for her? Removing her from the hubbub caused by the scandal with Sam could not be the sole reason. Her father hadn't concerned himself with the details of her life in the past. Why now?

A prick jabbed her finger. She flinched and brought the protesting finger to her mouth. *Rooster feathers.* That was the fifth time she'd stabbed herself with the sewing needle in as many minutes. Any more pokes and she'd turn into a modiste's pock-marked pincushion.

She sighed and tossed the embroidery onto the end table beside her chair. She needed a distraction, and needlework clearly wasn't the answer. Outside the window, the morning sun basted vast fields of wheat in a golden glow. Their tall stalks reached for the sky while heads thick with grain bowed under the weight. The farmers would soon reap what they had sown in late fall and grown over the winter. Odd how some things thrived in adversity while others succumbed.

A soft chuckle drew her attention back inside the railcar. Seated across from her, Mrs. Sommers had her nose plunged deep in the pages of *Cousin Mary*, the latest of Mrs. Oliphant's novels. She had read the author's *A Beleaguered City,* a collection of short stories featuring ghosts and the mystical. Interesting themes, but thankfully all fiction. She couldn't imagine dealing with the supernatural. Real life held enough drama.

She shifted in the overstuffed chair, and a twinge speared her back. She grimaced and rubbed at the complaining muscles. The lumpy, feather mattress had been most uncomfortable, and a head plagued with gloomy thoughts had only added to her misery. Sleep had been elusive as a loose dollar bill on a windy day.

"I'm a good listener if you have a need to talk."

She donned the mask she'd worn for years, the one that conveyed contentment. "I'm fine, truly. Just a little unsure about what will meet me at the end of our journey."

Mrs. Sommers lowered the book to her lap. "That's understandable, Meggie. You haven't seen your father since you were a small child. But he does write, does he not? Alma mentioned as much."

"His letters, when they come, are full of tales of life at the fort, of the beautiful untamed lands, but nothing about him. About what he likes. What he dislikes. I feel as if I'm going to live with a stranger."

"Just give it time. You will become close with your father before you know it."

They had a vast amount of ground to cover before that happened. First and foremost was an explanation of why he had abandoned her. Her childhood years, she could understand. An army fortification was no place to raise a young child. But later, when she was older and able to care for herself, he could have sent for her. She hinted at such in her letters back to him. Yet, year after year, her appeals went unanswered until she finally stopped asking.

"I'm having a reunion with my family as well," Mrs. Sommers said. "My sister and her eldest son offered to meet us during our layover in Chicago. We haven't seen each other in nearly a decade."

Her companion's face glowed with happiness, and her tone was giddy as a child anticipating a promised peppermint stick. At least one of them was excited about their trip.

She widened a smile that would surely put cracks in her face. "How nice. You must be looking forward to visiting with them after so long."

"Indeed, I am. Walter is quite the prosperous banker, so my sister's letters say. He has a lovely home in McCormickville, one of the wealthier sections of Chicago. He is handsome and witty, always has an amusing anecdote on hand...*and* he's looking for a wife."

One gray eyebrow lifted in speculation. Meg cringed. Oh no. She was not going down that flower-strewn aisle. Not any time soon, if ever.

She shot to her feet. "I believe I will stretch my legs and explore the other railcars. Perhaps a short walk will help ease my restlessness."

"Of course. Enjoy your stroll, Meggie. And remember, not everyone believes Mr. Holloman's accusations. Some of us know exactly how respectable you are and wouldn't hesitate to recommend you as a prospective wife to their bachelor nephew."

"Thank you, Mrs. Sommers. I appreciate your confidence in me." Though that confidence was misplaced. She had hurt Sam with her irresponsible behavior. Had shot a cannonball into Teddy's plans. She wouldn't do that to another man, especially one her companion treasured. It was best if she completed her penance in solitary confinement.

She made her way out of their Pullman car and onto the breezeway between the railcars. A rush of smoke-clogged wind tugged at her hair and scoured her eyes. Her throat seized with a need to cough. She held her breath and grabbed the knob of the adjoining railcar. As much as she'd like to linger and enjoy the passing scenery, doing so might put her health in jeopardy.

She pushed inside and shut the door behind her. While a bit warm, the air was free of pollutants. She stood there, drawing in deep, purifying breaths. Her lungs soon stopped screaming, and her tear-veiled eyes cleared. A few gazes turned her way but didn't linger. She smoothed her hair with a hand. Good. She must not be as disheveled as she felt.

Similar to her and Mrs. Sommers's Pullman carriage, this railcar had windows lining each wall. Unlike theirs, the windows were clouded with soot and void of curtains. Row after row of unpadded, wood benches paraded down each side of a narrow aisle. Sitting on them would be a chore, sleeping a nightmare. Her complaint of a lumpy mattress seemed trivial in comparison.

Dozens of heads bobbed with the sway of the

railcar. Midway down the car, a soldier sat on the edge of a bench, hunched over in the aisle. Muted sunlight spewing through a window haloed his golden mane and glistened on the buttons decorating his uniform. Her heart set to clickety-clacking. *Sergeant Hunt.* What was it about the man that had her all out of sorts?

She shook the soot out her skirts *and* her head and started down the aisle. She had come to stretch her legs and that was what she was going to do, regardless of the blockades.

"Decide before you bounce the ball which jacks you are going to grab," the sergeant said to the young boy squatting at his feet. "Pick ones that are clumped closest together."

The boy pointed to several metal objects scattered on the floor. "Like those three?"

"Exactly. Bounce, scoop, and catch the ball."

The boy executed a perfect jack throw. He beamed up at his mentor. "I did it. All three in one try."

Sergeant Hunt reached out and ruffled curly brown locks. "You sure did. Keep practicing. Before long, you'll be able to grab most of them in one try."

She smiled at the exchange. Sergeant Hunt and Teddy were as different as fire and ice. What she had first seen as sophistication had actually been pompous arrogance. Teddy would never give a child the time of day, much less lower himself to play with one. He'd often said children were to be seen and not heard. A part of her was glad he had called off their engagement. As a father, he would be cold and distant. She knew the pain of rejection all too well. She wouldn't want a child of hers to endure such torture.

In contrast, Sergeant Hunt was compassionate and

discreet. When he found her visiting with Orion the other evening, he had to know she had been crying. Her voice had been thick with it. But he didn't say a word. He had acted as if nothing was amiss. She couldn't have appreciated his thoughtfulness more.

The sergeant looked up and caught sight of her in the aisle. He pushed to his feet and stepped around the boy. "Keep playing, Matty. I'll be right back."

He closed the distance between them in two strides. His aroma met her first. Soap and sandalwood. Not the nauseating bay rum cologne Teddy had bathed in. Pleasing tingles played over her skin, and a breath lodged in her throat. She shrugged off the sensation. She was merely still chilled and winded from crossing the smoky breezeway. Nothing more.

"Is there something you need, Miss Myer?"

A stray lock poked out over his ear. Her fingers itched to comb it back in place. She wagged her head instead. "I just wanted to move around a bit. Stretch my legs. I'm not accustomed to sitting for such long periods."

"Train travel is tiresome. Once we arrive in Chicago, there will be a six-hour layover before we board the Santa Fe for Guthrie. We can have lunch and then take a long, relaxing stroll if you'd like. Enjoy some of the sights near the stationhouse."

"That would be nice. I'll take you up on that offer, Sergeant." She peered around him at the boy squatting in the aisle. "You seem to know your way around jack rocks."

Amusement danced in his eyes. "I've played a time or two. And you? Do you play?"

"I confess to sneaking off from my lessons with a

sack of jacks I *borrowed* from my older cousin Daniel."

"Borrowed?"

"Daniel was away at boarding school. I didn't think he would mind."

"A girl after my own heart."

The railcar lurched and tossed her forward. She collided into a wall of blue. Steadying arms wrapped around her. She pressed her hands against his chest, the wool of his uniform rough beneath her fingertips. Her blood heated. Her knees went weak. She lost her breath for the third time that day.

She followed a parade of buttons upward until they ended at a sun-tanned neck. The skin covering his chin and jaw was smooth and shiny. He'd recently shaven. She drew in a ragged breath. Sandalwood. Her new favorite aroma.

She slid her gaze upward, sliding over slightly parted lips and a slender nose. Gleaming pools of gold ended her expedition. They coaxed and taunted. Quicksand couldn't be any deadlier.

"Are you all right, Miss Myer? The railcar took a rather vicious pitch that time."

She wasn't even close to being all right. Her head swam, and her pulse raced like a thoroughbred on a track. It would take hours for her body to settle to a more sedate pace.

She pushed out of his arms and took a step back. "I'm fine. Thank you. Perhaps I should wait until we reach Chicago to take a stroll. Then my feet will find firmer footing." As would the rest of her.

His smile threatened to topple her rickety equilibrium. He gave a brief nod. "I look forward to joining you on that walk."

She turned and headed back down the aisle, putting some much-needed distance between them. Sergeant Hunt was definitely a distraction. Thoughts her father and Fort Dent were the furthest things on her mind. But was the wit-robbing sergeant a good diversion or bad?

Chapter Three

Buildings stretched to the horizon, blanketing either side of a wide roadway. Tall ones, brick ones. Ones with awnings over the door, others presenting huge display windows. And there was no shortage of people. They swarmed like ants along the boardwalks and rode in conveyances stuffing the street. He preferred his hometown of Mineral. No hustle and bustle. No noise. Just a quiet little town with folks who took their time and appreciated what life had to offer.

The wagon approached an intersection where a huge, three-story building of pink granite and red bricks claimed the entire corner. Steeply pitched, louvered roofs and an immense clock tower reached for the sky. Dearborn Station. He'd passed through the stationhouse on his way east. Didn't pay it much mind back then. Getting to Virginia consumed his attention.

The driver reined the mules to a stop at the curb, ending the teeth-rattling jar. While the cobbled roadways cut down on mud, the wheels bouncing over uneven pavers sure did take a toll on the body. Every bone and muscle cried out in protest. He rolled the stiffness out of his shoulders. A long soak in a hot tub would be nice, along with a cigar and a glass of whiskey. But such indulgences would have to wait. He had charges to see to. As General Myer would say, duty before pleasure.

He climbed down from the wagon and strode to where Private Dunn sat in the bed, watching over the trunks and the black stallion hitched to the back. Orion stood patiently, eyes alert and ears flicking back and forth as he took in every sound...of which there were countless and in varying degrees of intensity.

"I'm going to have you ride with the driver to the loading sheds, Dunn." He reached up and patted the horse's sleek neck. "See that the ladies' trunks and Orion are properly secured until the train to Guthrie arrives and we can get them loaded."

"Should I stay at the sheds and watch over everything, sir?"

"I think that would be best. I'll send food and drink out, so you won't go hungry while you wait." As General Myer often reminded him, "good commanders always attend to their troops first." He would be the General George Washington of this little squad.

Private Dunn nodded, his wrinkles deepening into a grateful smile. "Thank you, Sergeant. A meal would be mighty nice."

He wheeled around and headed for the carriage pulling to a stop behind the wagon. General Myer should be pleased with his performance so far. He had handled the unexpected situation with Orion to everyone's satisfaction. Had made certain Miss Myer and Mrs. Sommers traveled in comfort and had everything they required. There had been nary a hiccup in their trip. Maybe his future in the army had a chance after all.

He tugged open the carriage door and held out a hand. Dainty, gloved fingers pressed into his palm, sending pleasing jolts shooting up his arm. Warmth rifled through him. He stifled a groan. He'd best get a rein on his body, else that future might just go up in smoke.

Miss Myer descended the short debarking stairs and removed her hand. Blue eyes skimmed over him and then focused on the wagon drawing away from the curb. Good. She didn't seem to notice the flames that surely had to be rising from beneath his collar. His neck and ears burned from the heat.

"Orion made the trip through town without any mishaps," he assured her. "Private Dunn is taking him to the loading sheds and will watch over him until the train to Guthrie arrives. Your horse will be well taken care of."

Her lips wanted to smile. They lifted and fell, and then rose to half-mast. "I know Orion is in good hands. I just wish I could spend more time with him. Let him know I'm thinking of him. I suppose he will have to manage without me until we reach Fort Dent."

He wanted to be there when that happened. When she and her beloved animal finally reached their destination, and she could put all her worries behind her. Those pretty lips would unfurl into a brilliant smile. Her face would light up like the sun. He wanted that for her, and more.

Pudgy, gloved fingers waggled in the opening, followed by the clearing of a throat. Damn. Caught woolgathering again. Mrs. Sommers must think him a dimwit. He grasped the woman's hand and assisted her out of the carriage. She waddled past him, silent, except for one quirked eyebrow.

She joined Miss Myer on the sidewalk and shaded her eyes from the midday sun with a hand. "My, my.

What a spectacular building. There's nothing quite like this in Wisconsin, don't you know."

Miss Myer nodded. "It is remarkable."

Remarkable if one liked the flamboyant. He shut the carriage door and motioned to the awning-covered entrance. "If you please, there's a waiting room inside where you can freshen up. I'll see to getting us a table at the Fred Harvey restaurant."

"They have a Fred Harvey in the stationhouse?" That purple hat feather bobbed with her nod. "I read about them in the newspaper. The owner wanted to provide travelers with fine dining during their journeys. His exceptional meals come highly recommended."

"Indeed, they do," came a deep reply.

A tall, slender man, wearing a brown top hat and a neatly pressed tweed suit slithered to a stop beside Mrs. Sommers. His face was freshly shaven. His hair neatly barbered. Even his brogans sported a recent bootblack shine. The man exuded wealth from every pore. Gabe bristled. Money or not, the man had no reason to be weaseling in on their conversation.

He took a step forward, but before he could send the intruder on his way, the man leaned in and gave Mrs. Sommers a quick buss on the cheek. The woman's face lit up like a candle-studded Christmas tree.

"Walter," she pushed out on a breathless exhale. "You made it."

"Yes, Auntie Bea. I made it."

Gabe fisted hands at his side. Not an interloper then. But something told him not to let down his guard. The man's tone held a bit too much sugar, and his smile was clearly fake. He'd learned long ago that a wide, toothy grin often veiled a merciless evil simmering within.

Mrs. Sommers tipped her head to the side as if looking for something behind the man. "Where is Elizabeth? Is she not coming?"

Weasel put on a consoling look that didn't quite reach his eyes. "Mother sends her regards. She is heartbroken that she can't make it. Her rheumatism is acting up again."

Disappointment blinked behind glass lenses. "I am sorry Sister is feeling poorly. I was looking forward to visiting with her. Letters are nice, but a face-to-face meeting would have been lovelier, don't you know."

"She's just as unhappy as you are. I'm afraid you'll have to make do with me."

"There's nothing to make do about." A pudgy hand snuggled into the newcomer's elbow. "I'm glad for a chance to visit with my nephew. I haven't seen you since you entered the university."

"And I am just as eager for our visit." He lowered his voice. "Don't tell anyone, but you are my favorite aunt."

Mrs. Sommers gave his arm a playful whack. "I'm your only aunt, you scalawag."

A chuckle more suited to a pig grunted out. Beady eyes shifted and roved over Miss Myer, slowly, appreciatively, as if assessing her for a purchase. The urge to punch the man rolled through him. Gabe pressed his hands to his sides. He would be the gentleman soldier General Myer expected him to be.

"Walter, this is Miss Myer, the young lady I wrote about," Mrs. Sommers said. "Margaret, this is my nephew Walter Peyton."

The man doffed his hat. "Miss Myer. It's a pleasure

to meet you. Auntie's letters don't do you justice. You are much prettier than any angel."

Cheeks flushed with pink. "Thank you, Mr. Peyton. It's nice to meet you as well."

Irritation surged in his veins. What a cad. He would love to take the smooth-talking dandy down a peg or two. But right now, he had other more important tasks to attend to.

He moved closer, hand extended. "Sergeant Hunt, Mr. Peyton. I'm escorting the ladies on their trip to Fort Dent. I'm sorry to interrupt your reunion with Mrs. Sommers, but we need to go inside and get a table before the lunch session ends."

Peyton clasped and released his hand in one hurried motion as if touching him was repulsive. "Sergeant Hunt. There's no need for that. I've already secured a table and placed an order with the cook for an extravagant meal. I'll see to the ladies now. You can go about your *other* duties."

His gut clenched. Dismissed. Flicked away like a bug crawling on a sleeve. He would never be accepted in their fancy world.

A gloved hand tucked into his arm, the touch soothing and invigorating at the same time. "Sergeant Hunt can join us, can he not, Mr. Peyton? Surely adding another place setting will not be an imposition for such a renowned restaurant."

Gabe glanced down and met a sturdy blue gaze. No half-masted, pretentious eyelids for Miss Myer. She was as genuine as the Hope diamond. Images surfaced of her wearing a glittery satin ballgown and silver ribbons twined in her hair. With her in his arms, they would be the king and queen of the ball. He grunted under his breath. What was it about this sprite of a lady that had him wanting the unattainable?

He shook off the fanciful thoughts with a wag of his head. "I wouldn't want to impose on your meal or on Mrs. Sommers's visit with her nephew. I'll just join Private Dunn at the train sheds and find something to eat elsewhere."

Her hat feather became the tail of a furious cat, bouncing, wagging, flicking. "Nonsense. You are our escort. You will come with us where you belong." She cast a pointed look at Walter. "Don't you agree, Mr. Peyton?"

The man dipped a stiff nod. "As you wish, Miss Myer."

Peyton's mouth said consent, yet his eyes shot daggers of disapproval. He'd bet his last dollar the weasel itched to have him bound and gagged and impressed on the closest ship.

"Perfect." Miss Myer tugged on his arm. "Let's go. I find I am famished."

He fell into step beside her. It was nice of her to champion him, but her efforts were a waste of time. He didn't belong in her world. He was from a different class. No amount of spit-shine would change that.

****

Polished marble floors stretched to three archways that led to the waiting rooms, the ticket offices, and the Fred Harvey restaurant. Dozens of travelers swarmed the main chamber like bees in a hive. He fisted his saber hilt. More insect-like activity. Hopefully, he would blend in and avoid getting stung.

He aimed for the concierge desk. The ladies had disappeared into the lavatory to freshen up, though

Miss Myer didn't need any freshening. She always looked neat and composed. Unlike him. No matter how much effort he put into his uniform, something would be awry. A smudge on a button. Lint on a sleeve. Daily inspections usually earned him a loud and up-close verbal rebuke. He never knew a man's face could grow so red so fast. In a matter of seconds, Lieutenant Allen would resemble a tomato spoiling in the hot summer sun. One poke and he would explode. Comical. But he didn't dare let a smile cross his face, else he'd be assigned to permanent latrine duty.

Speaking of comical...he scouted the chamber. There was no sign of a beanpole wearing a brown top hat. Peyton must have gone into the restaurant to see about ordering another place setting for their table. He almost felt guilty about putting the man to the trouble. Almost.

He pulled to a stop at the concierge booth. A dwarf-like man stood on the other side, most likely on a box to give him some height. His chest barely cleared the top of the counter. He had a small head and short arms. In contrast, his hands were big as potatoes. He had to force his focus on the attendant's face and not on the sausage-like fingers gripping the edge of the countertop.

"What can I do for you, officer?" the man asked.

He pointed to the yellow chevrons on his sleeve. "Not an officer. Just a sergeant." For now. If this mission went well, in a few short months, he could be on his way to West Point and an embroidered second lieutenant's shoulder strap.

"My apologies, Sergeant. What can I do for you?"

He fished coins from his pocket and slid them

across the counter. "I'd like to have a chicken dinner and something to drink sent out to my trooper. He's at the loading sheds, watching over traveling trunks and a black stallion."

"Certainly. I can take care of that for you. Would you like to include a dessert? Harvey's cook makes a most delicious apple pie."

Dunn did like his sweets. The man had gone on and on about his Scottish grandmother's plum pudding. A dessert would be his way of rewarding the trooper for carrying out his duties without complaint.

He pushed another coin onto the counter. "That sounds nice. Add a slice of pie to his order. And a dollop of cream."

"Very well. I will see to it that your trooper is taken care of." Thick fingers scooped up the coins. "Will you be dining in the restaurant this afternoon, sir?"

He'd rather dine with Dunn out in the sheds than endure a meal with the mealy-mouthed Peyton. But Miss Myer had insisted. Besides, it was his responsibility to attend to his charges, no matter how distasteful.

"I am on my way there now."

"Excellent. Enjoy your meal, Sergeant."

A purple hat feather bounced over the swarming heads. He might enjoy part of his meal. The part where he could observe Miss Myer and her fascinating facial expressions. Every emotion played across her face and spilled from her eyes. Anger. Sadness. Guilt. She would fail horribly at the poker table where masking one's feelings was crucial to winning.

He angled across the chamber and met the ladies at

the entrance to the restaurant. A smiling blue gaze hailed him. He would never tire of being welcomed by such sunshine.

"Are you ladies ready to go inside?"

Mrs. Sommers nodded. "More than ready, don't you know. My stomach thinks I have forgotten how to eat."

He smiled at her quip and pushed through the door. The heady aroma of food rushed to greet him. On the way east, he hadn't had time to indulge in a warm meal. He and Dunn had to double-time in order to catch the train to Virginia. They resorted to slaking their hunger with dried venison and an apple.

He held the door open, and Mrs. Sommers and Miss Myer sailed past him. A young lady in a white service dress approached. She wore a pleasant smile and an eager face.

"Mrs. Sommers? Miss Myer?" she asked. At their nods, the waitress pointed to the other side of the room. "If you'll follow me, Mr. Peyton is expecting you."

He trailed the ladies as they wound through the linen-draped tables dotting the dining room. Nearly every table was occupied with people filling their bellies. He should thank Peyton for securing a reservation, otherwise they would have been waiting for hours to be seated. He grunted under his breath. Later perhaps, once he made sure this *extravagant* meal went through without a hitch.

They finally reached a round table tucked discreetly in the corner. Porcelain plates and silver utensils decorated a spotless white linen tablecloth. Sparkling stemmed glasses awaited filling from a bottle of wine sitting near one of the plates. Perfect. He could use a drink. Something to take the edge off what promised to be a tedious afternoon.

Peyton pulled out a chair and assisted Mrs. Sommers to the table. Gabe did the same for Miss Myer and then took the seat beside her. He tucked the linen napkin onto his lap and smoothed out the wrinkles. Mrs. Campbell's teachings thumped in his head. Do not play with your utensils or crumble the bread. Do not put your elbows on the table or sit too far back. Most importantly, do not talk loudly or boisterously. Hmmph. Proper dining would give a man dyspepsia.

The wait staff swarmed around the table, filling their glasses with wine and setting plates of steaming food in front of them. The savory aroma of meat rose from a round cut of beef sitting on a pad of bread and sprinkled with green beans and dark flakes. Another mound of mashed potatoes sat next to it. His stomach rumbled. He picked up his fork. No, he had not forgotten how to eat.

"What is this dish, Walter?" Miss Sommers prodded the medallion with her knife. "The meat looks most delicious."

"It is tournedos of tenderloin à la *lavoipierre*. The beef is sautéed in madeira and topped with truffles."

"Oh, my. I'm sure it will taste wonderful. The French create meals fit for a king, don't you know."

"Indeed." Peyton picked up his knife and fork. "Please, let your taste buds enjoy this royal indulgence."

Gabe resisted the urge to roll his eyes. Peyton acted as if he had prepared the meal himself. Pompous jackass. He cut into the meat and focused on filling his belly. The tenderloin melted in his mouth, its savory

45

juices bathing his tongue. Most delicious. But he wasn't about to admit such a thing to Peyton. The man's head was already two sizes too big.

The low hum of conversation and the clink of silverware swirled around them. Miss Myer appeared to be enjoying her meal as well. Her pretty mouth softened with each forkful, and he thought he detected a moan. It seemed there *was* a silver lining to enduring a meal provided by Peyton.

Before long, the last dollop of potatoes disappeared into his mouth. He set his fork on the empty plate and leaned back in his chair. His stomach sighed in satisfaction. Definitely a meal fit for a king.

Across the table from him, foppish arms flailed the air. "I tell you, Auntie; the man would not take no for an answer."

Mrs. Sommers dabbed at her mouth with her napkin. "He was that difficult?"

"Most annoyingly so. He went on and on about the merits of his product. Natural this and natural that. Debating him took all my skills, but I finally prevailed. He left the bank with a frown and an empty wallet."

Gabe grunted. Peyton appeared to have missed the lesson on talking quietly and without hand gestures. The man's braying would make a deaf man wince.

Unfortunately, the boasting continued, long and loud. Gabe took a prolonged sip of wine. There wasn't enough spirit in the glass to dull the ache caused by Peyton's incessant nattering.

"I say, Mr. Holloman made quite the mistake regarding you, Miss Myer," the weasel whined.

Her head came up, eyes going wide. "P-pardon me?"

"He should never have denounced you and called off your engagement." Peyton wagged a finger. "A most strategic misstep on his part."

Pink drained from her cheeks. "H-how is that, Mr. Peyton?"

"Because...Holloman's loss is now my gain." A pleased grin sliced into the weasel's face. "If you are of a mind to accept my suit."

"I-I...don't know quite what to say."

Gabe pushed out a soft snort. He did. NO. *Nada.* Not interested.

"You don't have to decide right now. I am quite willing to give you all the time you need." Peyton reached across the table and patted her hand. "You appear to be well worth the wait, my dear."

She pulled her hand away and rubbed her fingers as if they'd been scalded. Her mouth sagged. The sparkle lighting her eyes dulled. All the joy she had found with the meal had vanished. The damn skunk.

Mrs. Sommers beamed. "You won't find a more devoted man than Walter, Meggie."

"Thank you, Auntie. Your vote of confidence is most appreciated."

The man then launched into a sermon expounding on his merits as husband and provider. With each bray, Miss Myer's expression waned further. She sat still as a statue as if moving might shatter her bones. Anger climbed inside him. Any gratitude he felt toward Peyton vanished.

"Auntie told me you are not too keen on going to live with your father. I can offer you sanctuary should the situation there become unbearable."

Blue eyes glistened with tears. Her bottom lip

trembled. Damn the man. Could he not see how insensitive his words were? It was time to teach the donkey a lesson on good manners.

He concentrated on building a swirling warmth in his skull. His temples pulsed. His skull thrummed. He aimed his gaze at Peyton and the wine glass sitting next to his plate. Dandified arms flailed the air.

Wait for it. Wait for it. There.

Gabe gave a mental push. Peyton's wine glass tipped over as if struck by a dramatic gesture. A spreading river of red stained the tablecloth and dribbled over the edge and into the man's lap.

Peyton yelped and shoved to his feet. He mopped at his trousers with a napkin. "How clumsy of me. Mother is always admonishing me for talking with my hands."

Gabe clamped his teeth around a grin. *You should listen more closely to Mama.*

Peyton tossed a red-stained napkin onto the table. "This won't do. Please, pardon me while I go and clean up."

Not so fast. Gabe pushed again. As Peyton turned to leave, the tablecloth slid with him as if caught on a buckle. Dinnerware spewed off the table and clattered to the floor.

Mrs. Sommers darted to her feet, quick for a woman of her size. Miss Myer shot upright, eyes wide and mouth forming a perfect *Oh*. He could think of a million other things she could do with that mouth.

His mind filled with the image of General Myer, head shaking, lips pursed into a thin, disapproving line. His treatment of Peyton had been less than gentlemanly. But damn, it felt good.

Chapter Four

Meg paused and peered into the display window. Lace-trimmed bonnets dotted the shelf on the other side of the glass. Blue ones. Tan ones. Ones adorned with feathers, and others with tulle. The sight of such prettiness usually served to cheer her. But not today. Not after Mr. Peyton's talk of husbands and marriage and strained paternal relationships.

She wanted to like the man. Mrs. Sommers clearly adored her nephew, despite his overbearing and somewhat obnoxious behavior. But she just couldn't summon an ounce of fondness. She'd much rather remain a spinster than marry such a boor.

A uniform bedecked image dusted the glass. Tall with sandy hair and tawny eyes. His arm brushed hers, and tingles paraded up her arm. Sergeant Hunt brought forth feelings in her that she had never experienced before. Pleasing, yet confusing feelings. He was an enigma. A puzzle. One she itched to solve.

"See anything you like?" he asked.

"Um. No. Nothing in particular." She anchored herself on her parasol handle and resumed her stroll. It would be best if she focused on something other than the men clouding her life. Otherwise, she might fall off the ledge she teetered on.

Chicago swarmed with activity. Dozens of wagons and carriages rattled over the cobbled street. Double that number of people darted through the traffic and swarmed along the brick walkway running beside the road. The roaring din hammered at the senses. Loud and mind-numbing. And it was just the discord she needed to drown the clamor roiling in her head.

Sergeant Hunt seemed to sense her need for peace. He remained silent, walking beside her, offering protection from the crowd and from herself. She cut a glance at him. He had no trouble maintaining his composure in the face of adversity. He had been the buffering shore to Mr. Peyton's wild whitecaps. After the disaster with the wine glass and the spilled dinnerware, the efficient soldier had taken charge, directing the wait staff and ushering her and Mrs. Sommers to safety. If only she had such a keen presence of mind. Maybe she wouldn't have turned into a puddle under Mr. Peyton's barbed innuendoes.

A young boy raced down the sidewalk, pulling a small wooden wagon behind him. A younger child sat inside, hands clamped on the sides, his face beaming with excitement. One of the wheels hit a bump. The wagon tipped, then righted itself and careened forward. The little passenger squealed in delight and called for the older boy to go faster.

Sergeant Hunt chuckled. "Those two remind me of myself when I was a youngster at Seaton House. Full of energy and daring. I'd wager their parents rarely get a moment's respite."

Her heart sighed. "I should like to have a whole passel of them one day. Boys *and* girls."

"You'll need a husband to help keep them corralled. Mr. Peyton seemed eager to take up that role. Too bad he had to leave so quickly and end your opportunity to further his acquaintance."

Was that a hint of derision in his voice? Mr. Peyton had not been overly friendly with their escort. Or was there more to the sergeant's dislike? Jealousy perhaps? Her blood trilled at the thought. If he was envious, that meant he liked her, might even care for her as more than just a duty. A part of her wanted his attention. Another part reminded her of all the hurt that came along with caring for someone.

She adjusted the parasol to block a stubborn shaft of sunlight. "I must admit, I was rather glad he departed. His need to chatter about himself was a bit..."

"Obsessive?" The sergeant's sarcastic snort sliced the air. "If you ask me, the man got what he deserved."

She cut another glance at him. If she didn't know better, she'd swear he had instigated the toppling of Peyton's wine glass. "I do feel sad for Mrs. Sommers. She had been so looking forward to visiting with her family. I'm afraid the day didn't end quite the way she had envisioned."

Her companion had declined their invitation to join them on their stroll. Said she would rather digest her food in the comfort of a padded chair in the waiting room. She suspected to digest her disappointment as well.

"She did seem to be hoping for something to develop between you and her nephew."

She shrugged. "She is sweet to want more for me, but right now, all I want is to reach Fort Dent and see what kind of life I can build there."

"With your father."

A subject she'd rather not discuss. Not now. Not with raw emotions bubbling just below the surface where the least little provocation could send them spilling over. The spectacle in the restaurant had been more than enough embarrassment for one day.

They crossed under a banner hanging from a wire strung across the street. It advertised copper-riveted overalls for miners, farmer mechanics, and cattle raisers. A billboard pasted on the wall outside a pharmacy lauded a cure for a weak heart. She would need an entire case of the curative for her ailing ticker.

"Tell me about Fort Dent," she said, needing a change of topic. "You mentioned the town of Mineral, but nothing of the fort."

"What do you want to know?"

"What does everyone do for entertainment? Surely there is time for some type of recreation."

"The officer's wives frequently organize parties and the occasional ball."

"That sounds enjoyable. Do you attend?"

His expression hardened. "Enlisted men are not invited to such festivities. Only officers and their families attend."

Just as in the civilian world, the military had class lines that were not to be crossed. It was unfair and led to resentment. As the commander's daughter, perhaps she could change that.

"Not to worry," he added. "During periods of free time, which isn't often, the rest of us find entertainment in other ways."

"Such as?"

"Last summer, Sergeant Peck organized a mule race." His soft chuckle stroked her ears. "But this was no ordinary race. The riders had to face backward, *and* they had to ride bareback. It was quite the event."

She smiled for the first time since the lunch debacle. "I imagine it was. Did your mule win?"

"Unfortunately, no. The creature decided the creek was more agreeable than a hot, dusty trail. Nothing I did stopped him from diving in. It took days for my boots to dry out."

An image surfaced of him floating fully clothed in a creek. A laugh bubbled up from deep inside her. There was no need for a heart curative around Sergeant Hunt.

She twirled her parasol. "The same thing happened to Sam. We went for a ride, and his horse decided to take a dip in a pond. He managed to dive clear of the rolling mare but ended up soaked to the skin. We giggled over the incident for days."

"Who is Sam? I don't recall meeting anyone by that name at Meadowdale."

Her cheerfulness plunged back into the cold water. "He used to work in the stables at Meadowdale."

"Used to? What happened to him?"

Sam was another subject she had no interest in discussing. She pointed to a colorful cart parked at the corner. "Look. That vendor is selling ribbons. Mrs. Sommers mentioned she needed a pink one to replace one she lost. Let's see if we can find a new one for her."

As she angled for the street vendor, the toe of her boot caught on an uneven brick. She gasped and lurched forward. A steadying arm caught her waist, and she was pulled against a rock-hard chest. Heat spread under her ribs. Her head spun. What a potent man he was. From his handsome looks to his funny and caring spirit. She could easily fall under his spell.

He glanced down at the sidewalk. "The city needs to take better care of its walkways."

No. She needed to take better care of where she entrusted her feet…and her heart.

****

Gabe strode along the halted rail cars. The early morning sun glistened on the windows and set the panes to steaming. The train had rushed through the night, heading west. They would be pulling into the stationhouse in Mineral before long, and his mission would be over. He just had to get everyone safely through the next twelve hours.

He glanced over his shoulder at the head of the train. Crewmen buzzed around a wagon, shoveling coal from the bed and into the coal car hitched behind the engine. The only sound was an occasional shout of instruction. So far, so good. He'd learned from the conductor that one of the railcars held guards and a safe containing the payroll for Delaney's Mining Operation. Only a select few knew of its passage on the train.

He toed a rock across the yard. Dammit. The Santa Fe Railroad owners might as well have painted a bull's eye on their train. There wouldn't be robbers if information like a safe full of money remained a secret. It added a deadly complication to his assignment, one he didn't want or need. Unfortunately, there wasn't much he could do about it. He would just have to be extra vigilant until the train and his group parted ways.

He took in a quick lay of the land. Just south of the stationhouse sat the town of Augusta. A little hole-in-the-wall with a handful of buildings lining a dirt-packed roadway. A woman stood in the opening of a mercantile, plying a broom to what was most likely a never-ending battle with dirt. Two men kicked up puffs as they crossed the street. Dry weather appeared to have settled into Kansas with a vengeance.

Nothing moved in or around the caboose end of the train or along the expanse of track heading back the way they had come. All clear for now. Miss Myer had asked to visit with Orion during the layover, but he had vetoed that request. He didn't want her worrying over the real reason behind his refusal, so he merely said there wasn't enough time. She had given her usual pound of argument, and after seeing he wasn't going to budge, finally retreated into her Pullman car with a disgusted huff.

She was one perplexing lady. On the surface, she appeared to be female perfection. All composed and ladylike. She could tell a person off with a pointed look and a politely couched word. But inside, Lordy, was she a spitfire. She wanted what she wanted and wasn't going to let anyone stand in her way. Admirable and quite intriguing. If he thought he had a hair of chance, he might just see if there could be more between them. But that would be a mistake. She would expect honesty from him. Something he couldn't offer. He held too many secrets for that.

Besides, she made it clear she wasn't interested in any relationships. She had declined Peyton's offer of marriage quicker than a startled rabbit dove for cover. All she wanted was to build a life with her father. He could understand that. Were his father still alive, he would want the same.

Not seeing anything suspicious, he angled for the horse car. The door had been thrown open to let in the sunlight and fresh air. A soft whistling issued from within. He recognized the colorful Irish ditty. Private O'Connell had often entertained their squad with similar refrains to ease the monotony of the long, dusty patrol rides.

He braced his arms on the bottom of the opening and leaned in. The attendant stood near Orion's head, his red hair flaming in a beam of sunlight. Ned set a bucket on the floor, and the stallion dove in, sloshing water with his nose.

"Everything going all right, Ned?"

Green eyes flicked in his direction. "Fine and dandy, Sergeant. Just fetched himself some fresh water. The old bucket was getting a bit stale."

"Is he staying on his feed?"

"Eating every morsel and clamoring for more. He'll be a hundred pounds heavier by the time we reach Fort Dent."

"All your efforts are much appreciated, by me and by Miss Myer."

"She sure does love this fellow." Ned gave the horse's neck a pat. "Something I can understand. He's a gentle soul. Hasn't given me a wee speck of trouble."

"Miss Myer will be pleased to hear it. She wanted to come out for a visit, but there's not enough time on this stop. She'll be able to see him when we reach—"

The press of steel into his spine stole the rest of his words. He stiffened. Dammit to hell, what he feared most had gotten the jump on him.

"Hands in the air, soldier," came a gruff voice. "Slow and easy. Any fast moves and you'll be sleeping with the worms."

His pulse thudded in his ears. How many were there and where were they positioned? In his experience, criminals usually traveled in packs. Well-armed and well-coordinated packs.

"Take it easy, Mister." He inched his hands skyward. "No need to get an itchy trigger finger."

"Keep following directions and I won't have to. You there, inside the horse car. Come out where I can see you. Hands up, and no funny moves."

The Irishman hesitated, his gaze shifting from side to side as if weighing his options. There weren't any to be had. At least not yet.

"Just do as he says, Ned. Everything will be all right."

Ned shuffled closer, hands upraised, green eyes wide as wagon wheels. "We don't want any trouble, Mister."

"Too late, Irishman. Trouble found you."

Something brushed his waist, and then the scrape of his revolver being lifted from its holster rasped out. Anger reared up inside him. The theft of his manhood couldn't kick any worse.

He focused on building energy in his head. Orion's bucket would make for an effective projectile. If he could disable this gunman, perhaps he could get a jump on the others before they swarmed the train.

A shadow fell beside his and the robber's, and then another, and another. Four. Maybe more. Damn. Damn. Damn. One bucket wasn't going to be much use against such a horde. Besides, Ned might get injured in the process.

An image surfaced of a woman lying on the barroom floor, eyes vacant and blood pooling around her. His attempt to settle an argument over cards using his gift had caused an innocent to be hurt. He wouldn't let that happen again. Ever.

"That sure is a nice piece of horseflesh," the shadow to his left said.

"Uh-huh. Real nice," replied stick-up guy.

"You said you needed a new mount now that Sundance is getting old and slow. Why not take that one?"

Oh, hell no. Miss Myer would have apoplexy if anyone took her beloved horse. He wagged his head. "I wouldn't do that if I were you."

The pistol dug deeper into his spine "Not much you can do about it, soldier. Nothing, 'cept get a bullet in your back."

"Not me doing the doing. That horse is the property of General Edward Myer, commander of Fort Dent in the Oklahoma Territories. He'll hunt you to the ends of the earth if you take his prized stud." A bit of truth twisting, but still accurate if he knew his commander.

A nasty stream of tobacco juice splattered the ground near his boots. "He can look all he wants. There are plenty of places to hole up that an army general can't find. Just ask Geronimo about that."

Geronimo. The Apache who had evaded the army for decades. It sounded like the leader had a well-thought-out plan of escape. Not a good sign.

"J.J., you stay here and guard these two while we go help Rafe with the dynamite. Have the Irishman unload that stallion and get him saddled with Sundance's tack. We should have that safe blown shortly."

They had explosives. He couldn't let them go any further with their dangerous scheme. Miss Myer could be hurt, or worse. The pressure on his spine eased. It was now or never.

He shifted and twisted, grabbing for the gun. His attacker yanked out of reach. He lunged again. Something smacked the back of his skull. Hard. Pain exploded in his head, and everything went dark.

****

Muffled blasts sifted into the rail car from outside. Meg stilled and cocked her head. Was that gunfire? It sure sounded like it. Sam had given her shooting lessons one summer afternoon. He said she should know how to protect herself if the need ever arose. She would never forget the sound of that barking gun. It had been near deafening.

She lifted the window and stuck her head through the opening. Nothing moved at either end of the train.

"Is something the matter, Meggie?"

She pulled back inside. "I don't know. I thought I heard gunshots, but I don't see anything amiss out there."

Mrs. Sommers clasped a hand to her chest, eyes going wide behind her spectacles. "Gunshots? Oh my, could it be train robbers? I read about them in the newspapers. Horrible men who hurt innocent people and take their money and valuables."

She'd read about them as well. Hard, ruthless men with not an ounce of compassion or mercy. She crossed to the east side of the railcar. Before she could look out the window, the door blasted open, startling a gasp from her.

Private Dunn filled the doorway, his usually stoic expression cratered with worry. "Sorry to barge in like this, but the train is under attack."

Her pulse skipped. "I thought I heard gunshots, but I didn't see anything outside the window to the west. I was just about to look on this side."

"They're to the east at the far end of the train near the caboose. At least a dozen of them, if not more. Stay in this railcar. On the floor would be safest. I'll be right outside, standing guard. Lock the door behind me, and don't let anyone in except me or Sergeant Hunt."

She swallowed her last bit of moisture and rushed for the door. "Of course, Private. Stay safe."

He nodded and ducked out of the doorway. She shut the door behind him and threw the latch with a resounding click. Train robbers. Lord in Heaven above. Was Orion safe? What about Sergeant Hunt? As he'd exited the train after denying her request to visit with Orion, she had cast imaginary daggers at his back, wishing him all sorts of evils for his boorish behavior. She hauled in a calming breath. Her wishes had never been granted before. No reason to think that would change now.

"Oh, dear me. What will we do, Meggie?"

Mrs. Sommers's fretful tone dashed into her gloomy thoughts. She put on her most confident expression and pushed away from the door. "We'll do exactly as Private Dunn suggested. I'll come help you to the floor."

Before she could make it to her companion, an explosion rocked the rail car. The blast tossed her sideways. She grabbed for purchase and latched onto the curtain hanging at the window. It held her weight, but her momentum swung her against the wall. A dull pain stabbed her hip. She yelped and worked to get her feet under her. She finally steadied herself and let go of the curtain.

A few feet away, Mrs. Sommers lay sprawled at the foot of her chair, skirts tossed up and bonnet askew. Meg stumbled forward and knelt beside the woman. Blood seeped from a gash on her temple. Her spectacles were nowhere to be seen.

Pale eyelids blinked in confusion. "Wh-what happened?"

Meg fished a handkerchief from her pocket. "An explosion of some sort. It rocked the car and tossed you out of your chair."

"Land sakes."

"You must have struck your head. You have a gash that's bleeding." Meg pressed the wadded handkerchief to the woman's temple. "Here, hold this against the wound. Tightly now, so it staunches the flow of blood."

Though her hand trembled, Mrs. Sommers managed to take control of the bandage. "What about you, Meggie? Are you all right? Did you hurt yourself?"

"I'm fine. Just a bruise where I fell against the wall. Nothing to worry ab—"

The bark of gunfire blasted into her words. She yelped and launched at Mrs. Sommers, sheltering the older woman with her body. That barrage was close. Very close. Like just outside their railcar close.

A window shattered, and then another. Heart thumping, she tucked her chin to her chest and covered her head with her arms. She tossed a prayer skyward for Him to keep everyone safe. Surely her sins weren't so great that he would completely ignore her pleas.

After what seemed an eternity, the gunfire slowed and then stopped. She unfurled her arms and lifted her head. The silence was near deafening. Was the battle over, or just a hiatus? Only one way to find out.

She rolled off Mrs. Sommers and pushed to her feet. "I'm going to see what's happening."

Her companion wiggled to a sitting position. "It's too dangerous, Meggie. Just wait for Private Dunn or Sergeant Hunt to come."

After all that gunfire, they might never come. And she wasn't going to wait like a timid lamb for the slaughter. "I will be careful. Just a quick peek out the door to see if I can spot either of them."

She skirted a traveling trunk that had slid into the aisle. Mrs. Sommers's satchel had upended. Its contents dotted the floor. She tiptoed around linen handkerchiefs, a gold rouge box, a fan, and a silver flask. Spirits? Her companion might need a good, long nip after this calamity was over.

She reached the door and rested her ear against the wood. Coolness bathed her cheek. There was no sound coming from the other side.

"Private Dunn," she called out. "Are you there? Can you hear me?"

Only silence greeted her. Had he left his post to chase after the robbers? Or had a bullet taken his voice away? Her blood went cold at the thought.

"Private Dunn," she tried again, louder this time. "Is everything all right?"

More silence. She glanced back at Mrs. Sommers. Her companion sat on the floor, leaning against the chair, eyes closed, and the bandage pressed to her head. Her skin was pale, but not unhealthily so. With a little rest and tender care, she should recover just fine.

Meg turned back to the door and reached for the

latch. Her hand trembled. She clenched and unclenched her fingers. This was no time for cowardice. Someone might need her help.

She grasped the latch and slid the bolt clear. She moved her hand to the handle and inched the door open enough to peek through. The passageway between the railcars was empty. No Private Dunn. More importantly, no robbers with guns.

She pushed the door wider and stepped onto the landing. Something rushed in her periphery to the right. She turned and her heart froze. A dozen riders were galloping away from the train, the leader riding a familiar horse with a sleek black coat and flowing mane. Her knees buckled, and she reached for the handrail. Bile burned in her throat. They might as well have put a bullet in her heart as to take Orion.

Through a haze, she watched as the thieves raced away. Orion would be lost to her forever. She shoved steel into her spine. No, he would not. Sergeant Hunt would go after them. He knew how much Orion meant to her. He would rescue the horse from those polecats.

The acrid scent of smoke speared into her thoughts. She scooted to the other side of the breezeway, and her pulse took a nose-dive. Private Dunn lie at the foot of the short stairs with a small pool of blood spreading out from his left shoulder. His chest rose and fell in shallow draws. Praise be. He was alive. Bleeding, but alive.

Farther down the tracks, she could make out the bodies of two other men. One had a yellow stripe streaming down his trouser leg. *Sergeant Hunt.* A breath caught in her throat. Was he dead?

Private Dunn's arms and legs began twitching. His head rolled from side to side. He was coming around.

She clattered down the steps and went down on her knees beside him. A dark red stain circled a hole piercing his jacket. He had been shot, but not lethally so. A few more inches south, and he would be measured for a coffin. All he needed right now was something to staunch the bleeding.

She rolled up her skirt and exposed her petticoat. She gripped the hem and wrenched off a long strip. Most ladies she knew would faint at the sight of blood. She wasn't most ladies.

She quickly folded the cloth and pressed it to the bullet wound. Moist warmth seeped into the material and bathed her fingers. The bullet must have nicked a vessel. She leaned over and put her weight into stopping the flow.

Private Dunn groaned. Pale eyelids flickered and then rose. Bleary eyes focused on her. "Miss Myer. T-tried to stop them. Couldn't. Too many. Got shot…"

"Shhh, everything is fine. The train robbers are no longer a threat. They have ridden off."

His gaze rolled to the side. "Sergeant…Hunt? Is he all right?"

He tried to push up on an elbow, but she stopped him with a hand to his shoulder. "Don't try to move. Your wound is still bleeding."

"But I saw…they had him surrounded. H-he fell…then the shooting started. Don't know if he's…"

Dead? Her stomach knotted. Dear God, she hoped not. She needed him alive. Needed him to go after Orion. If she was honest with herself, she needed his unwavering strength to make it to her destination without shattering like the railcar windows.

She glanced at the far end of the train. "He's still

64

on the ground back near the horse car. I can't tell if he's breathing or not."

The soldier must have heard the worry in her voice. His hand covered hers on the makeshift bandage. "Go. See to him."

"But you need help—"

"I'm feeling stronger. I can manage holding the bandage on the wound. The sergeant may need you more."

Chapter Five

"Sergeant Hunt. Wake up."

Such an angelic voice. Sweetness tinged with loving concern. Had he died and gone to heaven?

"Please wake up, Gabe. We need you. *I* need you."

Fingers pressed into his shoulder and gave a not-so-gentle shake. The darkness began to ebb. Gray turned to white. He opened his eyes and met a pretty face etched with worry lines. She was concerned for him. Said she needed him. To keep her safe? Or was there more to her fear?

Miss Myer heaved a sigh. "Sweet Jesus, you're awake."

His head pounded. His stomach roiled. Awake, but reluctantly so. He turned his head a fraction, just enough to look around. A handful of people milled around, pointing to the train and wagging their heads. None looked threatening.

"Don't worry, the robbers are gone."

He tried to answer, but the words refused to ride up his parched throat. He coughed and then winced at the pain stabbing his head.

She glanced over her shoulder at a man standing behind her. "Get him some water. Now."

Bossy little miss. But she was alive and seemed to be unharmed. That's all that mattered. He pushed up on his elbows. His head swam for a few seconds and then settled to a mild doggie-paddle. Annoying, but manageable.

A few feet away, a man with a red bandana covering his nose and mouth lay sprawled on the ground. Blood stained the dirt around him. His chest was still. His eyes were open and staring skyward. Dead. Good. Especially if he was the thug who had cold-cocked him.

Blue eyes ran the length of him. "I don't see any blood. Where are you hurt?"

He swallowed what little moisture he had left and managed to croak an answer. "My head."

Her attention shifted to his skull. Her touch was gentle, almost caring. If he didn't feel like a beat-up old rug, he might enjoy it.

"There's no blood. Just a good-sized lump."

"Uh-huh. One of the thugs…cracked me…with the butt end of his gun."

"At least it wasn't a bullet. Private Dunn took one to the shoulder."

His blood went cold. Dunn? Shot? "Is he all right?"

"He's alive. Luckily, the bullet missed his heart and only pierced his shoulder. He lost some blood, but he should recover without issue."

"And Mrs. Sommers? What about Ned?"

"Whatever exploded rocked our railcar and tossed Mrs. Sommers to the floor. She struck her head and sustained a gash. It's nothing serious. She should be all right with a little rest. As for Ned, he is fine. He went to our railcar to help care for Mrs. Sommers and Private Dunn."

All good outcomes, considering the circumstances. But he preferred that no one got harmed at all. Not on his watch.

"The explosion came from a dynamite blast," he said, his voice becoming stronger and clearer. "The robbers used it to blow open a safe."

"A safe?"

"The train was hauling a mining payroll. The thieves wanted it."

"That's not all they took."

Her gaze shifted to the ramp leading up to the horse car. Color drained from her face. Her mouth sagged. He didn't have to look inside the railcar to know what caused her suffering.

"Orion," he said.

She drew in a long, raggedy breath and nodded. "I saw one of them riding him as they fled from the train."

Damn. Damn. Damn. Couldn't something go right in his life for once? He must be cursed.

Footfalls pounded closer, and then the water fetcher appeared. He handed Miss Myer a tin. She leaned over, her sweet scent filling his senses. Roses. A smell that would haunt him for the rest of his days.

Her hand settled at his back, fingers pressing heat into his spine. "Here. Drink this. Slowly, or you'll toss it back up."

She lifted the tin to his lips. Their eyes met over the rim. A connection formed between them like the charge in the air before a storm. Color stormed into her cheeks. She wasn't as indifferent to him she as might want to be.

He took a sip. And then another. Cool water bathed his raw throat. Not exactly what he wanted to slake his thirst or the ache in his head, but it would have to suffice for now.

She withdrew the tin. "That's enough. You don't want to overdo."

"Thank you. That helped." He shifted onto his left hip, preparing to rise. "I should be able to get up now and see if anyone needs help."

Fingers clamped down on his shoulder as if to hold him in place. "The town doctor has been sent for to tend to the wounded. You should wait here and rest until he can see you, too."

"I'm fine. I don't need a doctor." He didn't have time to be idle. People needed to be questioned, and plans needed to be made. The train robbers already had a good head start.

He shrugged out of her grasp and pushed to his feet. Pain throbbed in his skull and thundered down his neck. Bile rose in his throat. The spinning in his head resumed at full gallop. He moaned and leaned against the railcar for support.

Footfalls scrabbled in the gravel, and a hand closed around his elbow. "You don't look fine to me. You can barely stand. I would bet my last dollar you can't see straight either. How many fingers am I holding up?"

He squinted at her. Her image shimmered and danced. He blinked and blinked again. Damn slap-happy gunslinger.

"Hmmph. I thought so. You won't be much use to any of us if you collapse."

Collapse, his ass. He was made of stronger stuff than that. He shoved away from the rail car and forced oak into his wobbly legs. The spinning receded; his vision cleared. All that remained was a pounding in his skull. Nothing a tall glass of whiskey wouldn't cure.

"Two," he said. "You're holding up two fingers,

and one of them has a broken nail."

If eyes could spit venom, he would be a dead man. But he wasn't. And he had things to do. He glanced beyond her at the water fetcher. A gust of wind tugged at the green apron tied around the man's waist. A merchant of some sort.

"Are you one of the townsfolk?" he asked.

The man nodded. "Name's Frank Stoneman. I own the town mercantile."

"Do you have a lawman?"

"Augusta's too small. Can't afford one. A marshal comes through every three months or so. Won't be here again until next month."

Damn. If it wasn't for bad luck, he'd have none. "I need a horse and anyone from town willing to go after those thugs."

"The horse I can help you with, but I wouldn't count on anyone from Augusta volunteering to go. Nate Sloan's bunch is well known around these parts. Vicious men. Few will stand up to them." He rubbed his thigh. "As for me, I got a bum leg. Can't ride for long periods. I wouldn't be much help to you."

Nate Sloan. His enemy now had a name. He bent and scooped his hat off the ground. "Bring me that horse and two others, if you would. I'll see if any of the other passengers are willing to ride out after those men."

"I doubt you'll have much luck with the passengers either. Sloan's bunch killed the two men guarding the safe and three others who tried to stop them. Half a dozen others were injured in the gunfight."

More bad luck. Violence like that left people shell-shocked. It would take a miracle to convince them to go back into the fray. But he had to try. Miss Myer would have his head if he didn't.

Mr. Stoneman shoved hands into his apron pockets. "We sent a rider to Fort Smith. Might be best if you wait for the army to arrive and ride out with them."

"Fort Smith is a hard three-day ride from here. Sloan and his thugs will be long gone by the time a patrol arrives."

"Wish I had a better answer for you, Sergeant."

So did he. And so did Miss Myer. Tears shimmered in her eyes. Her shoulders and face slumped. The theft of Orion stole the very life from her.

He knocked dirt from his hat and tucked it on. His skull barked at him. He swayed for a moment and righted himself. He pasted on the most confident expression he could muster. "I *will* get Orion back for you, Miss Myer. One way or another."

Blue eyes studied him as if weighing the veracity of his statement. She swiped at her eyes and stalked toward a palomino grazing nearby. The gelding was saddleless and had the beginnings of a sway back. Sloan's old nag? The one he had boasted of trading for Orion?

She led the animal back to the horse car and held out the reins. "Hold onto him while I get my saddle."

"Your saddle? Why?"

"Because I'm going with you."

"Like hell you are."

She treated him to one of those looks like the ones Mrs. Campbell gave when he spoke nonsense. Eyebrows raised, and forehead tilted down.

"You are weaving like a sailor on a week-long drunk. There is no way you can go after those robbers by yourself."

"I don't plan to go after them alone."

"Exactly." She tossed him the reins and scrambled up the ramp and into the horse car. A few seconds later, she emerged, toting a sidesaddle.

Frustration rose inside him…at his weakness and at her unwavering determination to put herself in the path of danger. He blocked the base of the ramp. "I won't allow you to go with me."

"There's nothing you can do to stop me."

"I can hog-tie you to a chair with orders not to release you until the train gets back underway."

She stalked down the ramp, bootheels mashing into the wood. She stopped in front of him. The angle of the ramp put them at eye level, and hers were loaded for bear. "You *could* hog-tie me. But I *would* find a way to get free, and I *would* come after you."

An army mule didn't hold a candle to her obstinacy. "Your father will have me drawn and quartered if I allow you to go after those men."

Pink lips pulled into a taut line. "My father has no say in what I do. Now move aside and let me pass."

"You can't come with me, Miss Myer. It's too dangerous." He held out his hands and spread honey on his tone. "Please, give me that saddle."

She clutched the saddle to her chest. "Orion is everything to me. I would risk my life to rescue him from those thieves."

"I can't let you go; you know that."

Her face fell. "Please, Gabe. Don't fight me on this."

That was the second time she had used his given name. It sounded sweet passing over her lips. In any other circumstance, he would take advantage of it with a gentle kiss.

"My orders are to get you safely to Fort Dent. That won't happen if I let you go tromping off into the prairie. You heard what Mr. Stoneman said. Those thugs are vicious. They killed five men and wounded many more. They won't hesitate to shoot anyone who comes after them, including a woman."

Metal saddle fastenings jiggled with her agitation. "We don't have to confront them. We can just follow them until they stop. They have to rest at some point. Then we can send for help."

A sound suggestion. But still fraught with dangerous pitfalls. "It would be smarter to wait for that patrol from Fort Smith to arrive. Let them do the tracking and confronting."

"You said that could take days." Her voice cracked. "Orion doesn't have hours, much less days. The wind is starting to kick up. I'm no expert, but I'll bet the robber's tracks will be obliterated by nightfall."

She was right. But damn, he couldn't let her put her life in jeopardy. He was coming to care for her as more than a duty. Much more.

He reached out and grasped the saddle. "Let me see if I can convince a few men to ride with me. There has to be someone willing to go. I won't stop until Orion is returned to you. I promise."

She opened her mouth as if to argue, and then snapped her lips closed. She released her hold on the saddle. "Fine. Go and see what magic, if any, you can summon. I leave Orion's fate in your hands."

He wished he had that kind of magic. For now, he would just have to rely on his normal skills, the ones that could coax a frightened orphan to face monsters under his bed.

****

Only the whistle of the wind and the muffled clomp of hooves broke the silence. The prairie animals and insects had taken shelter from the brutal rays of the afternoon sun. Meg reined her mount around a patch of thorn bushes. Not an ideal time of day to be out and about. But she didn't have a choice. None of the townsfolk or train passengers would volunteer to join the posse to hunt for the robbers. Not a one. Cowards, all of them. Even her champion had earned a spineless stripe.

After failing to convince anyone to join him, Sergeant Hunt had decided to wait for the army patrol to arrive. He had refused to go after the thieves without reinforcements. He said the robbers were too numerous and too proficient with their firearms to go after alone. He wouldn't do her or Orion much good if he got killed. And he'd be damned if he was going to let her go with him. So she had done the only thing she could...slipped away on the palomino and rode off to find the robbers herself.

The horizon shimmered with waves of heat. She swiped at the perspiration trickling from under her bonnet. Her mouth was dry and thick as if she'd eaten a bowl of sand. Sweat pooled beneath her armpits and dribbled between her breasts, wetting the thin muslin of her gown. Hot. Breath-robbing hot. She let her foot drag through the tall grass. Clearly not a desert, but it sure felt like one.

She twisted and retrieved the canteen she'd found in the horse car. It most likely belonged to the attendant

Ned. He was a good man with a gentle touch and a quiet soul. He reminded her of Sam. Orion had flourished under the Irishman's care. She would find a way to reward him for his service once this fiasco was over. All she had to do was maintain a slow and steady pace, following the robber's trail until her quarry went to ground.

A shadow soared over the grass in front of her. She tilted her head back and scanned the sky. To the south, a black-winged scavenger rode the air currents, dipping and circling, looking for carrion. She grunted under her breath. *Not yet, buzzard boy. I'm alive and kicking and intend to stay that way.*

Speaking of looking for prey…there was no doubt in her mind that Sergeant Hunt would come after her once he discovered her missing. He was too smart not to figure out what she had done.

She had claimed to be feeling poorly and needed to rest. She waited for Mrs. Sommers to fall asleep before slipping out of the railcar and stealing like a fugitive to the horse car. Duplicity went against everything she held dear. But she needed a good head start in order to get as far from the train as possible before it resumed its westward trek. Once the sergeant caught up with her, and she knew he would, then his only option would be to push onward after Orion. If making that happen required lying and suffering in the late afternoon heat, then so be it. She would deal with the consequences later.

She uncapped the lid and lifted the canteen to her lips. A blast of air snaked across the ground, kicking up dust and debris and whipping at the tall grass. She clamped her mouth around an unladylike curse. The robbers' trail was already difficult to follow. If this wind kept up, their tracks would be wiped clean.

Sam had taught her how to track game. Well, tried to. Tracking was not an easy endeavor. It required a person's full attention. Watch for trampled grass. Watch for prints and droppings to appear in the bare spots. Watch for branches broken by the passing of prey. After a while, she had grown weary of the tedious task and sought other adventures. Now she regretted her impatience. Perhaps she could have learned one more tidbit that might help her track Orion.

Thoughts of Sam blustered in her head. How was he faring? Did he require the use of his tracking skills to find food? Did he have a warm, safe place to sleep? She had asked him to write and tell her about his new life, but he had declined. He said it would be best if they made a clean break. Her head understood, but her heart cried at the loss.

The wind finally let up, allowing her to indulge in a long drink of water. It was warm and a bit stale. But it would have to do. There had been no sign of a creek or a pond, and she couldn't risk going off course to look for a source to freshen her canteen.

As she twisted the cap back on, her mount gave a sickening lurch. The canteen slipped from her grasp and fell to the ground. She grabbed the horse's mane and clamped her leg around the pommel, fighting to hold her seat. Her heart thudded against her ribs. Getting thrown could be disastrous. Especially out in the middle of nowhere with no help for hundreds of miles.

She managed to remain in the saddle as the gelding righted itself. Other than a twinge in her neck, she was unharmed. Unfortunately, the animal didn't fare as providently. It began walking with a marked limp. She pushed out a heavy breath. Why, oh why did everything in her life have to be so laden with difficulty?

She reined the horse to a stop, unhooked her leg from the pommel, and slid to the ground. Muscles cramped from the prolonged ride cried out in agony. Her knees wanted to buckle. She grabbed the stirrup strap and held on, waiting for the pain to subside. An image emerged of tawny eyes spitting "I told you so." She shoveled bricks into her wobbly legs and released the strap. She wasn't buzzard bait, yet. Not by a long shot.

She hobbled to the horse's head and slipped a hand under the bridle. "Come on, old boy. Let's see what's wrong with you."

She led the palomino forward, watching as it moved. The problem presented itself immediately. The metal shoe on its right front hoof had come loose, causing the limp. She would never be able to refasten the shoe on her own. Best to just take the thing off. Twenty feet to the right, the grass parted around a small mound of rocks. Perfect. She could look for a long, thin one to pry off the shoe.

As they neared the rocky cluster, a warning rattle spiked the air. The palomino jerked sideways and yanked from her grasp. She made a grab for the reins, but the gelding took off, galloping and kicking up its heels. She raced after the animal, yelling for it to stop. The horse kept going, clearly unaffected by the loose shoe or her shouts. She pulled to a heaving halt. Damnation. Yet another coward darkening her life.

She clenched her hands and looked back to the east. Returning to the train would be the wise thing to do. The safe thing to do. While…she faced the sun hurtling for the horizon…continuing after the robbers on foot would be full of dangers like that rattlesnake. She could be hurt or worse. A chill ran over her. So could Orion. The palomino's unexpected bolt was a perfect example of what could happen out on the prairie.

Sunlight glinted on something metallic. It was the canteen she had dropped when her mount faltered. She kicked through the grass and plucked the canteen off the ground. There. She had water. She had eaten a healthy breakfast, and she had a good pair of legs. Well, good was a relative term. They still worked. That was all she needed to get to her destination.

She scoured the endless ocean of green. The telltale path of flattened grass was gone. Wind and time had allowed the fronds to straighten. She slung the canteen strap over her shoulder. There was no backing down now. Orion had been there for her when she needed him, and now, he needed her. She wouldn't give up on him. Ever.

She hiked up her skirts and angled for the southwest. That was the direction the robber's tracks had been leading all day. Common sense said they would continue on that path, heading for the mountains that bordered the Oklahoma Territories. Father had written about the Arbuckle mountains to the west of the fort and the numerous caves that had drawn silver miners centuries ago. There would be no shortage of places for the robbers to hide.

She pushed forward, struggling to put one foot in front of the other as the wind and grass whipped at her skirts. Fortunately, she wore sturdy boots. There had been no opportunity to change into slippers between the time Sergeant Hunt had vetoed her visit with Orion and when the shooting had started. It was a small boon amid a day of misfortune.

Rolling, green hills dotted with patches of brown stretched as far as the eye could see. A clump of trees here and there broke the monotony. The sky was just as vast with nary a cloud shattering the sea of blue. Blue. Like Sergeant Hunt's uniform. Was he all right? He had sustained a hard hit to the head which could turn deadly if not properly nursed. One of the workers at Meadowdale had perished after receiving a glancing kick from a horse. While the sergeant's deliberate inaction angered her, she didn't wish him ill or worse.

The longer she walked, the lower the sun sank. The sheltering insects began emerging and playing their nightly symphony. It wouldn't be long before the four-legged hunters started their prowling. She rested her hand on the gun tucked in her waistband. She needed the weapon more than the dead robber did. He was more likely to need a block of ice where he was headed.

Light turned to gray. Shadows disappeared. The temperature dipped, and her skin pimpled beneath the sweat-dampened gown. She folded her arms over her chest, fighting the shivers. She would not succumb to the cold. Or to the desire mounting inside her to abandon her trek. Every bone in her body screamed for a respite. Her muscles burned. Her head swam. The need to stop railed inside her. But she couldn't give in. She had to keep going. Had to find Orion. Her selfishness had put him in harm's way. If she hadn't insisted on bringing the stallion to Fort Dent, he wouldn't have been stolen, wouldn't be under the control of a merciless thief.

Aunt Alma and Uncle Edward had urged her to leave Orion at Meadowdale. When she refused, they had accused her of being headstrong and of using poor judgment. They said she was endangering herself and the horse by taking him with her. It was yet another reason she had to get Orion back. She had to prove her aunt and uncle were wrong about her, completely wrong.

Chapter Six

Winking stars and a quarter moon provided some light, but not nearly enough to follow the ribbon of trampled grass leading into the darkness. He gave a mental push. The flickering lantern drifted closer until it hovered a few feet in front of his horse. A risky move. Anyone could see the strange light moving of its own accord over the ground. But he had to chance being discovered. He had to find his quarry and find her fast.

Damn fool woman. What was she thinking? Going after Sloan's bunch was dangerous. Not to mention dealing with the hazards of the open prairie. The panic strangling his throat when he discovered her missing had subsided. As had the desire to push his mount into a life-threatening gallop. The only thing that remained was an unwavering determination to catch up to her. She had a good two-hour head start, most of which she had covered in daylight and with no infirmity to slow her down.

Unlike him. His head pounded. His eyes felt as if they were going to pop out of their sockets. But he had to keep going. Meg's life depended on it. He would find her, even if it killed him.

He had come to care for her. Not as a duty, but as a friend. And possibly more if she would allow it. She was an intriguing combination of strength and softness.

He wanted to learn more about her. Wanted to court her once they reached Fort Dent and see if that spark in her eyes meant more than just irritation at his refusal to do her bidding.

His horse snorted and shied to the left. He gathered the animal and scanned the area to see what had caused the skittishness. Lantern light spilled over a lump of pale muslin nested in the grass. *Meg.* Was she hurt, or…?

No. She couldn't be. He wouldn't allow it.

He vaulted from the saddle and rushed to her side. She lay curled on her side in the grass, eyes closed, mouth partly open. Her chest rose and fell at an even pace. She was alive. But was she unharmed?

He settled the lantern on the ground beside her and went down on his knees. No blood or gashes marred the material of her gown. He skimmed a hand along her arms and legs. There were no awkward bends or lumps indicating a broken bone. Neither her face nor any of her exposed skin showed any signs of bruising. Not harmed on the outside then. But what about on the inside? Had she taken a spill and suffered an internal injury?

He glanced around. Only an empty sea of grass danced in the circle of light. Where was the palomino? Had it dumped her and run off? He loosened the laces tied under her chin and slid the hat off her head. She moaned but remained still. He gently pressed on her skull. No lumps or bumps. No sticky mats of blood. Only silky smoothness. He heaved a sigh of relief. No sign of a head injury. Hopefully, she was just sleeping the sleep of sheer exhaustion.

A chilly gust of wind whipped over the grass and

swirled around them. Gooseflesh crawled over his skin. Cold. And going to get colder as the night wore on. A fire would be nice but finding wood on the prairie would be nearly impossible, and he didn't want to leave her alone while he searched. Slender shoulders shuddered beneath his fingertips. If her body chilled too much, she could fall ill. Not on his watch. He shrugged out of his jacket and tucked it around her chest and shoulders.

Her head rolled to the side, and she moaned again. Eyelids fluttered open. Blue eyes landed on him and went wide as saucers. She sucked in a breath and bolted upright. "S-Sergeant Hunt."

"Yes, it's me. What the hell were you thinking?"

He said it softly, without malice. He understood why she had snuck off on her own. He would have done the same had they taken something he loved. But damn, her distrust stung.

Her chin went up in that lovely show of defiance he was coming to admire. "No one else had the courage to go after Orion."

"I told you I would get him back for you."

"Yes, but only after the army arrived. The thieves' trail would be long gone by then."

"So you decided to go after them yourself. Alone. What if you'd met up with a wild animal or someone harboring ill intentions?"

She unearthed a pistol from the folds of her skirt. "I would have shot them. I'm not an empty-headed imbecile. I knew I needed protection, so I took this from one of the dead robbers. He didn't need it any longer."

Smart, as well as beautiful. Was it any wonder he

found her so fascinating? "What happened to the palomino?"

Her expression waned, and she looked away. Ah, a weakness. She wasn't as competent as she claimed to be.

"Did it dump you?"

She turned back, eyes flashing. "No, it didn't dump me. The creature stumbled and then started limping. I dismounted to see what was wrong and discovered a loose shoe. When I led the animal over to a mound of rocks to fix it, a rattlesnake spooked him. The mule-headed lummox yanked free and ran off."

He held back a laugh. No sense poking an annoyed hornet. She appeared to have suffered enough from her ineptness. "How long did you travel on foot?"

"I don't know. More hours than I could count. I walked until I couldn't go another step." Her shoulders and face slumped. "I guess you're going to take me back."

His heart went out to her. He knew firsthand the sharp bite of failure. It hurt for days on end.

He picked up the jacket that had fallen to her lap and tossed it around her shoulders. "As much as I'd like to return to the train, we can't go back. The Santa Fe has already resumed its journey west. We'll just have to continue to Fort Dent on our own."

"What about Orion?"

"As I said before, it's too dangerous to go after Sloan's bunch without help."

"But we know the direction they're heading. It would be easy to pick up their trail again." She stuck a hand through the gap in the jacket and pointed at the darkness. "I bet they're heading for the mountains to the southwest. The Arbuckles, Father called them."

"They could be. However, it's wiser to let the army go after them. Mr. Stoneman said he would inform the patrol of Orion's theft when they arrived in Augusta. They will see to it your horse is returned to you."

Tears pooled in her eyes. She drew in a long, shuddering breath, clearly fighting for control. "What if...they don't?"

"Don't what?"

Pale eyelids briefly closed over the shimmering blueness. A tear slid free and trickled down her cheek. "Find him. Return him to me."

"That won't happen."

"H-how to do you know? There are so many uncertainties, so many things that can go wrong. What if they never find him? What if something happens to him, and he can never be returned to me?"

Her anguish stabbed into him. He wanted to pull her into his arms, offer comfort. But he wasn't sure if that would help or make things worse. So he took the safe route and snugged the jacket ends back together. "You just have to have faith. Trust in something bigger than yourself."

"Orion is the only thing that has ever been there for me. I trust him." A sob rabbited from her throat. Tears she'd held in check streamed down her cheeks. "I-I can't do it, Gabe. I can't go on without him."

She fell toward him, and he gathered her in his arms. Her body shook with deep, heart-wrenching sobs. Fingers dug into his shirt as if searching for a handhold.

"Shhh." He breathed over the top of her head. "Everything will be all right. Orion will be returned to you safe and sound. You'll see."

"H-he's everything to me. My happiness. My hope. My reason for living. I-I have to get him back."

He'd give anything to be loved so deeply. To have someone's soul bleed for him like that. "We'll get him back. I promise."

Her sobs continued unabated. Clearly, words were of no solace. He shifted to a more comfortable position and just held onto her. She shuddered with hurt. Painful, agonizing hurt. His heart bled with her.

Another gust of wind whisked around them. With Meg as his blanket, he barely noticed the chill. Tendrils of her hair lifted and tickled his face. He remained still, ignoring the urge to unfurl his arms and scratch. Meg needed the anchor of his arms, and he needed her warmth.

Minutes passed. Or was it hours? Her trembling abated. Her crying slowed, leaving only shallow hiccups of grief. He wanted to give the top of her head a consoling kiss. But such a show of intimacy, no matter how benign, might spook her. She was already troubled enough.

"Better?" he whispered.

She leaned away and swiped tears from her face. "I-I think so."

"A good cry always helps. Gets the poison out, Mrs. Campbell says."

A frown crimped her brow. She rested a hand on his chest. "My tears have soiled your shirt. I'm so sorry. I'm usually stronger than that."

"You're exhausted and dealing with the loss of something you love. It's understandable."

She tilted her head and peered up at him with those deep blue eyes a man could drown in. "Thank you. I may not show it, but I truly am grateful for all you have done for me."

"I'm glad to be of service. Why don't you rest for a while? It will be morning soon. I'll keep watch until dawn breaks."

She lifted a hand and gently touched the side of his head. "What about you? Your head must surely be hurting. I can see the pain in your eyes."

"I'll be fine. It doesn't hurt as much as it did earlier."

"Liar." Her tone held no censure, just a soft caress of concern.

He merely smiled. She was a wonderful lady. Kind and caring. He wanted to love all the hurt and loneliness right out of her.

He held up an arm. "Rest now. I will be strong for the both of us."

She leaned into him and snuggled against his chest. Her warmth seeped into his skin, into his soul. He could stay like this forever.

Her fingers toyed with a shirt button. "You're a good man, Gabe Hunt. I'm glad my father assigned you to be my escort."

Gabe. He closed his eyes, savoring the closeness. He had found her. Now what? The wise thing to do would be to ride to the next town where they could catch another train or secure stagecoach passage to Fort Dent. But her devastation over Orion's theft plucked at his heartstrings. She needed that horse. Needed the love and security it brought her.

And he wanted her to have it.

****

Her body hummed. There was no other word to

describe the sensation rumbling through her every time her chest rubbed against the muscular back in front of her. Which was often, considering how their mount blundered over the uneven terrain.

She rode on the horse's rump, fingers clamped on the rolled blanket tied to the saddle. Not a firm purchase, but she wasn't about to anchor her hands on the tempting waist in front of her. That would be akin to putting a match to dry kindling.

At first, she'd held herself ramrod stiff. But the tiresome ride had worn down her defenses, and she eventually just let the rollicking movement take over. Every collision sent pleasing jolts hurtling through her. Her pulse raced. Her blood heated. She clamped her teeth around a groan. Torture. Pure torture. If Gabe sought to punish her for rushing headlong into the prairie after Orion, he couldn't have picked a better method.

Gabe. After spending the night in his arms, she felt as if she could think of him that way. He had held her when she most needed comfort. He hadn't scowled or spewed admonishments at her failed rescue attempt, even though she deserved it. He just sat there, arms providing an anchor against her exhaustion and despair. Once this fiasco was over and they reached Fort Dent, she would make it up to him. She heaved a sigh. Just another chit added to her growing pile.

She glanced at the sun sitting halfway to its resting place for the evening. Another few hours and darkness would descend. Would she and Gabe spend another night together, wrapped in each other's arms? They would stay warmer that way. But lordy, such intimacy would play havoc with her body. She was more likely to go up in flames than freeze.

The horse lurched sideways. Her fingers lost their grip, and she grabbed for the only other anchor available…Gabe's waist. She kept her seat, but not her wits. Muscles rippled beneath her fingertips. Strong and sinewy. Tingles ran up her arms. Her head spun. She couldn't prevent a moan from slipping past her lips.

Unlike her, the horse collected itself. Gabe twisted and glanced over his shoulder. Tawny eyes drilled into her. "Are you all right? Do we need to stop?"

Only if the halt included a dip in a creek to cool her smoldering body. She pulled her hands from his waist and gripped the blanket with a good, firm grasp. No more inadvertent touching. "I'm fine. There's no need to stop."

"Good. We should be nearing the town of Lasley soon. We can enjoy a solid meal and sleep on real beds for the night."

They would sleep in comfort. But what about Orion? Was he sleeping? Had he even been allowed to rest or were the thieves pushing him beyond his limits?

A piercing cry drew her gaze skyward. A black speck dotted the blueness. It was amazing how far birds of prey could see as they soared overhead searching for prey. No movement would go undetected. If only she had such an ability. Her quest to find Orion would be faster and easier, and much less worrisome.

"A comfy bed sounds nice." Despite her efforts, despair tinted her tone.

"I hear the concern in your voice. Orion will be fine. From what I saw, he's made of strong stuff. He will come through this ordeal without any problems."

"I know you are right, but I can't help but worry."

He reined the horse around a small stand of juniper. "Let's take your mind off your worries. Are you familiar with the town of Lasley?"

She wagged her head. "The farthest west I've been is Ohio. I know little about anything beyond there."

"I found out about the place when my patrol rode through just after I joined the army. Lasley formed along the Arkansas River nearly a hundred years ago and slowly built up over the years. In order to trade with their neighbors on the other side, they constructed a pontoon bridge to span the waterway. It's the closest crossing point for miles."

Crossing point? She sat straighter, her spirits perking. "Could the robbers have gone that way to use the bridge?"

"If I were them and needed to get to the mountains in a hurry, I would have ridden for it."

"Are you saying what I think you are saying?"

"Partly. Since we're already heading that way, I figured it wouldn't hurt to see if they rode through and when. Then we can decide what to do next."

Her heart sang. "Oh, Gabe. You don't know how much this means to me."

"Don't get too excited. They may have gone in a different direction."

"But there's a chance they did go there."

"A slim chance, yes."

"I'll take those odds." She squirmed with the itch to urge the horse into a faster pace even if it meant being tossed more often against Gabe's backside. "How much longer before we arrive in Lasley?"

His chuckle spilled over her. "You sound like my sister. Patience is not her strong suit. It's not much farther. Maybe another hour or so."

An hour too long. She needed something new to focus on...for several reasons. "Tell me about your sister...Sally, I think you called her? How did you two come to live at an orphanage?"

His back went ramrod stiff. He remained silent, clearly chewing over an answer.

"If it's too difficult to talk about, I understand." She too had things she would rather not let see the light of day.

He pushed out a long, uneven breath. "No. It's all right. It's just not a pretty story."

"Pretty is for fairy tales. Go on with your story if you want. If not, we can talk about something else." Preferably not her twisted fable.

The horse dove into a shallow gully and scrambled up the other side. She bounced against Gabe's backside, and for the umpteenth time, heat fizzed inside her. She closed her eyes and imagined herself immersed in a chilly bath. With bubbles. She liked bubbles. They reminded her of happier times when Mama was alive, and life floated along on a tranquil breeze.

The ride evened out, and she leaned away, putting what little distance she could between her and that tantalizing back. Little good a firm purchase on the blanket had done. She smoldered...hands, feet, and unmentionable parts that had never even twitched until Gabe Hunt came into her life.

"I told you earlier my parents had passed," he said. "My father was killed by a wild boar when I was four. Sally was just a baby. My mother died a year later of a lingering lung illness. We were sent to live with our only other relative, my mother's brother."

"How difficult that must have been for you at such a young age."

"It would have been easier had Uncle Morris been a decent man. But he wasn't. He was very abusive. He beat me for the smallest infraction and often for no reason at all."

His voice crackled like old paper. If she could see his face, it would surely be crinkled with misery. She wanted to offer comfort as he had for her, but something told her he needed to vent. Get rid of the poison, as his orphanage mother would have said.

His shoulders rose with a deep breath and lowered with his exhale. "The worm ignored Sally, only providing the least care possible to keep her alive. I tended to her as best a five-year-old could. She's a strong girl. Survived when I thought for sure she wouldn't. As we got older, uncle would abandon us for days, sometimes weeks on end. We had to fend for ourselves. When Mrs. Campbell learned of our plight, she came to our rescue and brought us to Seaton House."

"Where is this uncle now?"

"He never came looking for us, so either he didn't care that we were gone, or he died. Sally and I were happy either way."

His tone held no emotion. Just emptiness. While she didn't wish ill on anyone, this slimy Uncle Morris of his didn't deserve to draw breath. But saying so would only darken the clouds hovering over him. She focused on the positive in his story.

"I don't know your sister, but if Sally is anything like you, she met her new life head-on and never looked back."

"Sally had a rough start, but once she realized she could trust everyone at Seaton House, she blossomed."

She smiled. "I can't wait to meet her and all the others at Seaton House. You did promise me a visit."

"I did. And I'm sure everyone will enjoy meeting you."

His tone and the tension in his back eased. Good. Her basket of troubles was full enough for them both.

"What about you?" he asked over his shoulder. "Your aunt seemed to be a decent lady. She was quite concerned about you going to Fort Dent."

Only because a bad outcome would reflect on her as a guardian. Alma Wheaton was all about image. She shrugged. "She was nice enough."

"But she wasn't your mother."

He understood her on so many levels. With family. With Orion. The shared bond covered her like a blanket. As hard as she tried to shield herself, Gabe Hunt had broken through, had made her feel again. Did she dare consider opening her heart and experience something new, something exciting?

Chapter Seven

"I'm sorry to disappoint you, ma'am. But the only strangers I saw come through this morning were a family headed west in a mule-drawn wagon. No riders and no sign of a black stallion."

The owner of the livery where they had dropped off Gabe's horse for stabling had suggested they speak with Elias Hammock about any strangers riding through Lasley. The elderly man lived in the brick house at the end of the street, closest to the bridge. Mr. Hammock was the town sentinel, watching the comings and goings from his rocker on the front porch. He had no reason that she could think of to lie.

"Is there anyone else in town who might have seen them?" She motioned to the bridge spanning the waterway. "We believe they were headed this way to cross the river."

"I doubt it. I'm the early bird in Lasley. Been sitting out here since just before sunup. Gout keeps me up late and wakes me early. I got a clear view of the bridge from my porch. Unless your riders passed through during the wee hours when I do manage to get some sleep, I ain't seen 'em."

Her heart sank. She was certain the train robbers had come this way. Would have bet money on it. Gabe had warned her not to get her hopes up. But she had. Now, the sunshine warming her insides had vanished.

Gabe extended a hand. "Thank you, Mr. Hammock. We appreciate you taking the time to speak with us."

"My pleasure, Sergeant. Sorry I wasn't much help." He shook Gabe's hand. "Daylight's almost gone. You planning on staying the night in Lasley?"

"We are. Do you have any recommendations for a clean but reasonably priced place to eat and has rooms for the night?"

White wisps bounced beneath the brim of a brown fedora. "Try the Lasley Hotel. Mick runs a tidy establishment. Has good food and decent beds. Fair prices, too. It's just across from the livery."

Gabe nodded. "I saw the place when we rode in. Thank you again, sir."

"Happy to help." Mr. Hammock tipped a finger to his hat. "ma'am. You have a restful evening."

How could she have a restful evening knowing the distance between her and Orion grew greater by the minute? Her beloved horse could be enduring gross mistreatment at the hands of those gun-toting lunatics. She had to put her exhaustion in a pocket and keep going. Resting was for weaklings.

She grabbed a handful of skirt and wheeled around. Footfalls thumped behind her, and then a long shadow joined hers on the dirt-packed roadway.

"I can tell by the way your boots are ironing the ground that you're upset about the bad news and want to rush back into the hunt. But we can't. My horse has to rest, and so do we."

"I don't need to rest. What I need is to find out where those dastardly thieves took Orion."

"I want that more than anything as well. But it

would be a waste of time and effort to try and pick up Sloan's trail in the dark. Not to mention dangerous. We can eat, get a good night's sleep, and then make plans in the morning."

"If this *plan* involves giving up and going to Fort Dent without Orion, then count me out."

"You are being unrealistic. The robber's trail has gone cold and finding it is going to be nearly impossible, even in the daylight."

Her insides churned. "But we can't stop looking. We just can't."

"Tonight, we can. We have to. If we don't take care of ourselves, mentally and physically, then we will never find Orion."

He was right. They had to rest and restore their depleted reserves, else they would be forced to stop when they couldn't go another step, just as she'd done out on the prairie.

She slowed her headlong charge. "Fine. But come sunup, we will make plans for renewing our search for Orion. Agreed?"

He remained silent as if chewing over an answer. Her blood started to simmer. "Sergeant?"

He finally nodded. "We will discuss our options in the morning."

His vague answer did little to instill confidence. But there wasn't much she could do about it. She could barely put one foot in front of the other, much less engage in a mental battle. Once she had her strength restored, she would be ready to fight. Gabriel Hunt would not know what hit him.

The last of the light from the setting sun burnished the buildings facing the street. Red, white, and blue bunting draped many of the windows and doors, and one large banner extended rafter to rafter across the street. She hadn't noticed the decorations before. Her attention had been too consumed with talking to Mr. Hammock.

Gabe pointed at a two-story, clapboard building just ahead of them. "There's the Lasley Hotel."

Her stomach sank, and she pulled to a stop. "It says Lasley Hotel and *Saloon*. I can't go in there. There will be drunkards and gamblers and ladies of the night."

"It's also a hotel. One we can afford with our dwindling funds."

Muted conversations and the tinkle of piano music drifted through the doorway, left open to invite customers to partake of the entertainment. She squinted, straining to see what lurked inside. She could make out the silhouette of a man standing at a long, wooden counter. Several other men sat around a table, playing cards and gaming away their hard-earned money. There was no sign of any half-naked women hovering about, ready to ply their trade, just as Sam's dime novels had portrayed.

She sighed. What was she so worried about? The incident with Sam had dented her reputation. And traveling alone with Gabe had taken a hammer to it. Going into a house of ill repute couldn't damage something that was already demolished.

"Well?" Gabe asked.

She smoothed the bun at the back of her neck. After a night spent on the open prairie, her hair must look like a rat had clawed through it. A nice hot bath would do her hair and skin wonders. Hopefully they *had* a tub.

She gave a nod. "I suppose this hotel will do."

"Good. Let's go inside. As Mrs. Sommers would say, my stomach thinks my mouth forgot how to eat."

His attempt at levity did little to lessen her unease. Her insides frothed like waves in a storm. But she had no choice. It was this place or the cold, unforgiving prairie.

She hiked her skirts and sailed into the hotel. The smell of whiskey and cigar smoke whacked at her. The threesome sitting around the table looked up, took her measure, and returned to their cards. The man sipping on a glass of whiskey at the bar didn't even acknowledge her entrance. She released her skirts with a sigh of relief. The place appeared to be peaceful and clean. Nary a splotch of dirt marred the neatly swept floor.

The windows were bare of curtains. There were no rugs or tapestries. The only embellishments were two large oil paintings hanging on opposite walls. Both were landscapes depicting the muted browns and greens of the rolling prairie. She'd seen enough of that scenery for a while.

Behind the counter hung several neatly printed signs. Shave and bath $.15. Rooms and a square meal $1.25. Her stomach grumbled. Food sounded wonderful, square or otherwise.

A man wearing a blue and white striped apron emerged from an archway and angled behind the counter. A red beard stretched to the middle of his chest, a stark contrast to the balding pate glimmering in the lamplight.

"What can I do for you folks?" the man asked.

Gabe eased past her and went to the counter. He

gave the bartender a nod. "Good evening, sir. I'm Sergeant Hunt, and this is my sister. We'd like a meal and two rooms for the night."

Sister. It was sweet of him to try and maintain her reputation. Few would question a woman traveling unchaperoned with her brother. Unfortunately, they had passed the point of preservation days ago.

The bartender picked up a cloth rag and swiped at a wet spot on the counter. "The meal 'tis no problem. But the room…I'm sorry to say there's only one left available. The town is that full for our Founder's Day festival."

A festival. That explained the decorations. It would be a fun-filled day for the townsfolk. Not so much for her and Gabe.

"I would be recommending Mr. Barton's place down the street to you. But he said just this morning that all his rooms were taken."

The bartender spoke with a noticeable lilt. Scottish, perhaps? He sounded much like the stable master at Meadowdale. Even resembled him with his red hair and brawny stature. Hopefully, his temperament was less fractious.

Gabe slid several bills across the counter. "One room will do. I can sleep in the stable. What's on the menu for supper?"

"Chicken, summer squash, coffee, and apple pie. Best pie this side of the Mississippi."

Her mouth watered. Apple pie was her favorite. She might just eat dessert before the entree. Who would rebuke her?

"Send up two plates…Mr.?"

"McCormick. Mick McCormick at your service,

Sergeant."

"Pleased to meet you, Mr. McCormick." Gabe pointed to bottles lining the shelf behind the counter. "Do you have any wine?"

Mr. McCormick nodded. "That I do. I recently purchased a case of 1885 Latour claret for Founder's Day. A great year for wine, so the French say."

"Perfect. Send up a bottle and some glasses."

"And your luggage, sir?"

"No luggage. We left in a hurry and are traveling light."

The bartender didn't bat an eyelash. He'd probably heard all sorts of fabrications in his profession.

He handed Gabe a key. "Room ten. Up the stairs and to the right. Last door on the left. My boy Ian will be up shortly with your meal and some hot water for washing."

"Thank you, that will be much appreciated. By the way, have you seen any strangers ride through town in the past day or so? A gang of about seven men led by a man called Nate Sloan."

She leaned closer. Now the conversation had some meat to it.

"I've heard of Nate Sloan and his bunch. Dangerous men. Why is it you ask?"

"They stole something of ours, and we want it back."

"Tis not a group you will be wanting to go after, Sergeant."

"We're not planning to confront them. We just want to know where they might be headed. Have you seen them?"

"Not recently." Mr. McCormick scooped up the

money. "If I hear any whisperings of their whereabouts, I'll be sure to let you know."

****

The splash of water drifted across the room. Meg wanted to wash up before eating. Get the trail dust off, she said. *Meg*. He felt as if he could think of her that way after all they had been through together. They shared the same devotion to those they loved. Would sacrifice anything to keep them safe. It was a connection he felt right down to his core.

What sounded like boots hitting the floorboards behind him rang out, and then came the shush of fabric. Was she undressing? The thought of honey-gold locks framing a velvety naked body lit a fire in his groin. He stuffed down a groan and focused on the darkness outside the window. He and Meg could not be *that* close. At least not until they said their "I do's." For now, he had to think of her as the sister he had claimed her to be.

A gentle breeze sifted through the open window and cooled his heated skin. He pushed out a relieved breath. With any luck, he would make it through this intimate meal without making a fool of himself.

He glanced down at the small table nestled under the window. A platter of baked chicken and steamed yellow squash sat in the middle, accompanied by two smaller plates holding wedges of perfectly crusted pie topped with a mound of cream. His mouth watered. *This* was a hunger he could sate.

He picked up the bottle of wine. A nice red claret. Costly on their meager budget, but necessary. Meg needed to rest. Hopefully, the spirits would help her relax and forget about her worries. Hell, he could use some numbing himself.

He poured wine into two glasses. "Are you just about done? Supper is getting cold."

"Just about. I need to get these…" The soft thump-thump of footfalls teased his senses. He couldn't stop from turning his head.

She had her back to him with her arms stretched over her shoulders as she attempted to refasten the buttons at the back of her dress. Pale skin peeked through the open folds. His fingers tingled with the desire to knead that pearly flesh.

"Need some help?"

The words rushed out before he could stop them. What was he thinking? He barely had a rein on his body as it was. To get that close would send him over the edge.

"No. I think I…" She gave a little hop and managed to fasten the top button. "There. That will do."

She turned, and blue eyes fused with his. Red climbed up her neck and flooded her cheeks. She hefted her chin and stalked toward him. "A gentleman would have kept his gaze averted."

He pulled a chair away from the table. "Never said I was a gentleman."

She gave a soft grunt and settled on the seat. He took the other chair and tucked the napkin on his lap. The soft glow of lantern light brushed her skin with golden strokes. A more lovely dinner partner, he couldn't imagine.

He picked up a knife and held it over the chicken. "Leg or breast?"

She formed a moue with her mouth and said, "Neither." She then snagged the dish of apple pie and set it on top of her empty dinner plate.

"A lady would save dessert for last," he teased.

Blue eyes twinkled. "I never claimed to be a lady."

Touché. He smiled. "You, my dear Meg Myer, are every bit a lady, even with your hair tousled and dirt on your face."

She patted her hair and took on a clearly contrived look of concern. "Is it so very messy? I thought I had tamed it."

"Only a wee bit messy." He picked up the other dish of pie and set it in front of him. "Let's enjoy ourselves, shall we? After all we've been through, we have earned the right to eat dessert first if we want."

"A man after my own heart." She spooned a healthy portion of pie into her mouth. Her eyelids drifted closed. Her face took on a dreamy look. Would she make the same expression when they made love?

He shook off the notion and picked up his fork. "Good, huh?"

"Delicious." Eyelids rose, and a serene blue gaze met his. "Mr. McCormick was right. This is the best pie this side of the Mississippi."

He dove in and devoured the pie in four forkfuls. Sweet, tangy goodness bathed his tongue. Delicious, indeed. If the mess hall cooks baked half as good as this, he'd be a hundred pounds heavier.

Once they were done with dessert, he filled their dinner plates with chicken and squash. Only the sound of clicking utensils broke the quiet as they focused on filling their bellies.

A short while, and a cleaned plate later, Meg leaned back in her chair and dabbed the corner of her mouth with her napkin. "Mmm-mmm. That was devilishly scrumptious. I haven't eaten that much since Sam left."

"The stable boy you mentioned during our stroll in Chicago."

She rubbed the yellow string tied around her index finger. Her eyes took on a faraway look…a little happy, mostly sad. "Christina wasn't much of a companion, so I turned to Sam for fun and adventure. Over the years, we became good friends."

She cared for the guy. Maybe even loved him. Jealousy rose inside him.

"We were close," she said. "Very close. But there was never anything romantic between us. Sam was the brother I never had. The companion I needed in an atmosphere of coldness."

Envy shifted to sympathy and understanding. "You never did tell me what happened to him."

Her gaze drifted to the window. All the enjoyment she'd found with the meal left her face, leaving only sagging sorrow. "I happened to him."

She said it so softly he had to strain to make out the words. His insides twisted. The last thing he wanted was to make her sad. "You don't have to talk about him if you don't want to. I understand."

She wagged her head. "You should know what happened. Perhaps it will better explain why getting Orion back means so very much to me."

"I don't need any more explanation than what you have given."

A shimmering blue gaze fell on him. "Yes, you do. You deserve to know the full truth, especially if you are going to put your life in jeopardy going after Sloan and his bunch."

"Fine. Go on then...but only when you are ready."

He picked up his wine glass and sipped slowly, giving her time to gather herself. Whatever she had to say was not going to be easy. He would just wait and let her decide when and how much to divulge.

The mantel clock ticked off the seconds while Meg worked at folding her napkin. She lined the edges just so and smoothed out the folds until she had a neat and tidy square. She set it on her plate and looked up. Her eyes were clear, her expression intent. She was ready.

"You may have gathered from Mr. Peyton's remarks at lunch that I was once betrothed. Teddy Holloman and I were to be wed this past spring."

He hadn't been surprised by the news of a possible betrothal. Meg was too lovely and vibrant to be a spinster. "I did surmise as much. Peyton brayed about the loss being his gain."

She fingered the handle of the fork resting on her plate. "A month before the wedding, Teddy told me that after we married, we would be moving to New York City to live. I would be going to a strange city, far away from everyone and everything I had ever known. I was devastated."

He could understand that. Every time he left Mineral, a piece of his heart stayed behind.

"I stewed over the news for days," she continued. "Worrying and wavering over wanting to call off the wedding to going through with it. I finally went out to the stable to seek advice from Sam. I began to cry. He held me, letting me get the sadness out of my system. Teddy came in and found us together."

Uh-oh. He could guess the rest.

Tears glistened in her eyes. "Teddy wouldn't listen

to reason. He called off the wedding and left. I never saw him again. Uncle Robert fired Sam. Said if he ever saw him again, he would send for the law. After that, Orion became my anchor. He was the only thing that helped me through what was the most horrific time in my life, next to losing my mother."

The sadness staining her voice dug into his heart. He reached across the table and grasped her trembling hand. "I'm sorry you had to go through that, and it explains how very valuable Orion became to you."

"I couldn't have gone on without him. Everyone turned against me. I was maligned and ostracized. So were Aunt Alma and Christina. When no invitation came to the Thurston's annual spring ball, Alma wrote to my father and insisted he take me in."

That explained the rush to collect her from Virginia. He gave her fingers a comforting squeeze. "I wish I could wave my hand and wipe away all your torment. You didn't deserve to be treated so unkindly."

She gave him a watery smile. "Thank you for your kind words. They mean a lot coming from a man like you."

"A man like me?"

"You are decent and dependable."

If she only knew the truth, she would put a fork in those words. He shrugged. "I do my best to treat others as I would want to be treated. It's not always easy."

"Well, you do a wonderful job, and I admire you for it. Not everyone can be as honorable."

She admired him. Did he dare hope there could be more between them? Mrs. Campbell often said, "Hopes and dreams create the future." A future with Meg would be wonderful and bright. He grunted under his breath.

He hadn't made a fool of himself. He was just fooling himself.

****

She stopped in the doorway and held onto the jamb. Other than Gabe turning to face her, nothing moved in the dimly lit hallway or on the landing at the top of the stairs. All was quiet…well, as quiet as a saloon could get after dark. The soft tinkle of piano music and the low hum of conversation drifted up the staircase. It was much tamer than she had imagined. Perhaps she would survive a night sleeping above the impiety after all.

Gabe stood in front of her, holding onto his hat. A few crumbs dotted his jacket. Probably from the flaky, but oh-so-yummy pie crust. She reached up and brushed them away. Tawny eyes pierced into her. Heat burned in her neck and rose into her ears. She lowered her hand and curled her fingers into a ball at her side. Why did she always act before thinking? That gesture was far too intimate for their platonic relationship.

He cleared his throat. "Thank you. I seem to attract dirt and crumbs no matter what I do. My lack of tidiness gives my lieutenant apoplexy."

It was kind of him to make light of the issue. She wanted to slink back behind the door and melt into a pile of embarrassment. Instead, she gave a laugh that sounded forced even to her own ears. "My aunt always says I am a mess waiting to happen."

"We are two peas in a pod, it appears."

"I suppose we are."

He smiled and snuggled his hat on his head. "I should be going. You need to rest. I'll be sleeping at the stable across the street if you need anything. Just have

107

Mr. McCormick send word to me."

She didn't want him to go. Didn't want the lovely night to end. Their time together had been relaxing and cathartic. Being around Gabe was like being with Sam. Only different. More exciting. More stimulating, in a most pleasing sort of way.

"Thank you for the meal and the company," she said. "It was just what I needed."

His gaze drifted to her mouth. Was thinking of kissing her? Her pulse hopscotched. Having his lips on hers would be a delicious topping to the evening, like a dollop of cream on a slice of apple pie.

He leaned forward and pressed a gentle kiss to her lips. Soft and quick, yet oh-so blistering.

"Good night, Meg. Sleep well."

Meg. He said it with reverence. With affection. Did he care for her? She briefly closed her eyes and savored the feeling. Her lips tingled. Her body ached. She wanted more of what his kiss promised.

She pressed a finger to her lips. "What was that, Gabe?"

His expression darkened. He rolled his head back and sighed. "That was…a mistake. I apologize. It won't happen again."

A mistake? Surely not. It felt genuine all the way down to her toes.

Before she could respond, a shout plowed up from the stairs. More bellows joined in. Then came the bark of gunfire. She froze, her mouth going dry. A gunfight. Was she going to die before she could ever truly live?

Gabe stepped between her and the staircase. "Get back inside."

Her ears heard him, but her feet seemed to be tone-deaf. They refused to cooperate. Another gunshot rang out. She cringed, and a gasp escaped her lips.

Gabe snagged her waist and gave her a firm, but gentle shove. "Inside, Meg. Now."

She braced her sagging spine and with Gabe's support, managed to scuttle backwards into the bedroom. Once inside, he released her and unholstered his pistol.

"Take cover by the bed."

She wobbled for a moment and then found her balance and her wits. She scrambled for the other side of the bed and squatted. Her head whirled. Her heart pounded against her ribs. She anchored her fingers in the bedcovers. Guns and whiskey were not a good combination. Any altercation could get ugly quick. This one sounded like it was on its way to being particularly nasty.

Gabe moved to the doorway, pistol in hand, and craned his head around the jamb. She wanted to call out to him. To warn him to be careful. But the grip of fear refused to allow any words past her throat. All she could do was send a silent prayer skyward for Him to keep them safe.

Something thudded into the floor near her feet. Her breaths ceased. Her body went numb. She stared at the spot, waiting for the tiny iron monster to shatter through the wood. Nothing came. She fed her lungs with a breath and then another. She had dodged that bullet. Would she continue to be so lucky?

A few minutes later, the shouting and gunfire diminished and then silence descended. Her racing pulse slowed. Her frozen muscles thawed. She unfurled her fingers and pushed upright. "I-Is it over?"

"Sounds like it. I'm going down and check to be sure."

Her heart skipped a beat. "Gabe, no. You could be hurt."

He glanced over his shoulder. His expression showed none of the fear he surely must be feeling. It was nearly strangling her.

"I'll be fine," he said. "Lock the door behind me, and don't open it until I come back."

He disappeared into the hallway, and panic clawed at her throat. What if something happened to him? She couldn't go after Orion without him.

She scurried to the door and peeked around the jamb. He had reached the top of the stairs and was about to descend into the hell below. She opened her mouth to call him back. Lamplight shimmered on the barrel of his pistol. She snapped her lips closed. She was being silly. Gabe was a trained soldier. He could take care of himself. She would help him most by heeding his advice.

She pushed the door shut and threw the bolt. Despite her efforts to remain strong, her body trembled. She leaned against the jamb for support. She needed Gabe. Not just to help her find Orion, but for afterward as well. Living in a strange place and dealing with a father she knew nothing about would be easier if she had a friend to lean on. Someone to talk to. Gabe would be a wonderful friend. If not more.

Did she want more? Did he? She touched a finger to her lips. That kiss certainly said he did. Once all this was over and they were back at Fort Dent, she would like to see if anything might develop between them. Her feelings were certainly headed in that direction. She ignored the little voice screaming in her head. The one that said this could have been her father's plan from the start.

The faint thud of boot heels sounded from the hallway. A breath lodged in her throat. She waited, heart thudding.

Knuckles rapped on the door. "Meg, It's me. You can open the door. It's safe now."

Thank the Lord. She pushed the bolt free and opened the door. Gabe stood on the other side, looking hale and healthy. She let go of the breath she'd been holding and backed away from the doorway. "What happened? Why was there gunfire?"

He trailed her inside. "Some drovers got into a fight over a card game. Started shooting at each other. Mr. McCormick settled the ruckus with his shotgun and sent them all packing. There shouldn't be any more problems tonight."

"Are you certain?"

"As certain as I can be in a place like this." He glanced around the room. "Do you still have the pistol you took off that dead robber?"

"Yes, it's in the dresser drawer."

"Good. Put it under your pillow where you can get to it quicker if need be." He angled for the door. "Now, try and get some sleep. Tomorrow is going to be a long day. You need the rest. I'll come back at first light and wake you."

He was leaving. She would be alone. Unprotected. Her luck would only last for so long. If another fight broke out, a bullet would surely find its way through the floorboards. Talons of terror clawed at her insides. She bolted forward and snagged his arm. "Stop, Gabe."

He halted and turned. "What is it?"

She swallowed around the lump clogging her throat. "I-I don't want you to stay in the stable tonight. I want you here...with me."

Hard lines formed around his mouth. "I can't stay with you, Meg. You know that. Our traveling alone together is bad enough."

"I don't care. My reputation is already in tatters. What's one more pulled thread?" She squeezed his arm. "Please, Gabe. Stay here for the night. You can make a pallet by the door with the blankets from the bed. No one else will know but us."

"Secrets like that have a way of getting out. I don't want your name further dragged through the mud because of me."

"I don't give two hoots about my name. What I care about is staying safe. While I know how to handle a pistol, when fear takes over, I'm more likely to shoot myself in the foot than stop an intruder."

"I doubt that. You are strong and resourceful. I've seen it for myself."

Not as strong as she wanted to be. But she could be resourceful. She put on her most miserable expression, one that would make Christina proud. "I won't get the rest you say I need. I'll be up all night, waiting for another outbreak from below. Please, Gabe. For my peace of mind."

"You are one persistent lady. All right, if it will help you sleep better, I will stay here tonight."

She let go a relieved breath. "Thank you. It will definitely help."

He gave her hand a gentle pat and then peeled her fingers away from his arm. "I do need to leave, though.

Just long enough to get my things from the stable. That will give you some privacy to prepare for bed. Is that all right with you?"

"Yes. As long as you promise to return."

"I promise." He snagged the room key from the bureau. "Just put a blanket over by the door. I'll let myself in and make a pallet to sleep on. There's no need for you to get out of bed."

"Hurry back." She cringed at her wheedling tone. She wasn't usually so weak and needy. A good night's sleep should put her back on an even keel.

Chapter Eight

A beam of moonlight slipped through the curtains, taming some of the darkness. The fire in the fireplace had dwindled to glowing orange embers. He ought to get up and add more wood. But he just couldn't summon the energy. Besides, he didn't want to disturb Meg. When he returned from the stable, she had tossed and turned for a spell but seemed to have finally settled down for the night.

Not so for him. He'd made a quick stop at the bar before coming up...a shot of whiskey to help tame the churn in his belly. Bedding down in the same room as Meg was a seduction he didn't need, especially after that kiss, chaste though it had been. His body still burned with a need to finish what he started. To his relief, temptation slumbered peacefully in the bed. Now if he could just get his worrisome thoughts to retire.

They had no idea where Sloan and his bunch had gone and locating their trail would be nearly impossible in the vast untamed territories. His head told him General Myer would expect him to bring Meg to Fort Dent where she would be safe. His commander could then use his influence and power to find Orion. His heart told him Meg would buck against such a thing. She would crisscross the entire Oklahoma territory before she asked her estranged father for help.

Dammit. Two options, each making someone he

respected and cared about very unhappy. He groaned and rolled onto his side. Not much he could do about it now. It would be best if he just got some sleep. Maybe after a good night's rest, he could come up with a plan that would satisfy everyone.

Soft breaths drifted across the short distance. Good. Meg needed the rest. So did he. Yet sleep was elusive as a rabbit in a briar patch. Even with a blanket folded under him, his body screamed at the cold, unforgiving floor. He could do with a diversion. Something to take his mind off his aches and the enticing lady sleeping a few feet away.

He gathered energy in his head. His temples pulsed. His skull heated. He gave a mental push. His boots rose and hovered just off the floor. He pushed again. The pair walked to the foot of the bed, wheeled around, and headed back. Too tame. He increased the stream of energy pouring from his head. The boots launched in a rollicking polka. Now that was more like it.

Hop. Turn. Left foot. Right foot. Hop again. He enjoyed dancing, once he got the hang of it, that is. Mrs. Campbell said he danced like a newborn colt, all legs and feet. It took a lot of practice and numerous stubbed toes, but he finally mastered the intricate maneuvers.

The waltz was his favorite. Gliding over the dance floor with his partner tucked in his arms, dipping and twirling, their bodies moving as one. It was exhilarating and sensual at the same time. Nimble Miss Meg would float over the floorboards like a swan across the water. He would pull her close, feel the rise and fall of her bosom against his chest. Dancing with her would be heaven. Pure heaven.

One boot dipped too far and thumped the floorboards. The other followed suit. Their thuds echoed against the walls. He winced and looked at the bed. The mound of bedsheets twitched. A soft whimper wafted across the short distance. *Gripes.* His tomfoolery had disturbed her sleep.

He shut down the flow of energy, and his boots settled on the floor beside the dresser. Another whimper pealed out, louder and more frantic this time. The mound on the bed convulsed as if possessed.

"No. Not him."

A scream raised the hairs at the back of his neck. He bolted upright and rolled to his feet. The floorboards were ice cold. He ignored the chill and padded to the bed. Her eyelids were closed. Her chest rose and fell in short draws. Distress crinkled her pretty face.

"Please. I need him," she whispered.

Was she dreaming of Orion? She really did love that horse. Not finding the animal would kill her spirit. It was already wrecking her sleep.

A gasp rang out, and then eyelids shot open. Eyes shimmering with fear locked with his. Her pale skin melded into the whiteness of the pillow.

"D-don't," she muttered. "Please don't hurt him…"

"Shhh. It's all right, Meg. It's just me."

She blinked and blinked again. The fog of sleep cleared from her eyes. She glanced around the room and then back at him. "A-Are they gone?"

"Who?"

"The robbers."

The moonlight faded, and darkness overran the room. She gave another terrified gasp. Poor little bird.

Nightmares were horrible hazards of the night. She needed some light to chase away the darkness.

He fumbled for the matches he'd seen on the bedside table. There should be a candle planted in a holder beside them. She had placed them there in case there was a need for light. She was more resourceful than she gave herself credit for.

He found a match and struck it on the wall. A golden flame burst from the tip, providing enough light to see by. He set the flame to the candlewick. It caught, and soft yellow light painted the room.

He blew out the match and settled a hip on the side of the bed. "See. There's no one here but us. You were just having a nightmare."

"It seemed so real. I heard footsteps."

What she heard was his foolishness. He patted white-knuckled fingers clamped around the sheets. "It was just a dream. Go back to sleep. There are still a few hours left before day breaks."

"I don't think I'll be able to sleep." Slender shoulders shuddered. "Not after that dream."

"Was it about Orion?"

She flicked a pink tongue over her lips and averted her gaze. "Sort of."

Thoughts of his lips pressed to hers emerged, hot and fast. He shouldn't have kissed her earlier. But she stood there in the doorway looking so inviting. He couldn't stop himself. This time he would.

He dragged his hand away. "Fill your head with happy thoughts of Orion and your reunion with him. You will fall asleep in no time."

"I c-can't."

"Sure, you can. You do believe we will find Orion,

don't you?"

"I hope with all my heart that we will."

"Then focus on that. A positive heart heals all wounds." Finally, he could put one of Mrs. Campbell's oft-repeated sayings to use, even if he didn't always put much stock in them. He started to rise, but her fingers caught his, stopping him.

"Don't go, Gabe. I need to have you close."

The distant sound of thunder rumbled through the window. An early morning storm was brewing, in more ways than one.

He shook his head. "I can't stay with you like that, Meg. I'm disciplined, but not that disciplined."

"You didn't have any trouble holding me out on the prairie."

"That was different. You were exhausted and needed to be watched over."

"I need to *feel* watched over now. For my peace of mind." Her fingers pressed into his palm. "Please stay. You can rest on top of the covers. I'll remain underneath."

"Meg…"

"Please. I can't shake the images from that dream." She pulled in a breath and let it go on a ragged exhale. "It wasn't about Orion. It was about you. The robbers had surrounded us and were going to kill you."

She was worried about him. Because she cared about him, or because she could lose her best chance at getting Orion back?

"I'm fine." He squeezed reassurance into her fingers. "Healthy as a mule."

"Just stay with me for a few minutes. We can talk. Maybe I'll be able to fall back to sleep."

His sister didn't hold a candle to Meg's cajoling. He shifted and leaned back against the headboard with his legs stretched out on the bed. He folded his arms across his chest, confining his desire under a firm hold. "Very well. What do you want to talk about?"

She turned on her side and faced him. Blue eyes captured his. "Tell me about my father."

Didn't expect that. He cocked his head to the side and studied her. He loved watching the myriad of unconstrained emotions play across her face. "Don't you know everything there is to know about him?"

One side of her mouth tipped down. Her shoulders went up in a shrug. A perfect example of irritation and puzzlement.

"I know next to nothing about him. I haven't seen him since I was three years old. He writes, but he doesn't share his thoughts or his feelings. It's as if he's conversing with a stranger."

"Perhaps he doesn't know what to say."

"I'm his daughter. You'd think he would find a way."

"Put yourself in his boots. He is the commander of a large fortification of fighting men. He has to give orders and hand out punishments without prejudice, without emotion. All relationships must be kept impersonal."

"He must have some friends. People he can talk with on a personal level." She levered up on an elbow, one eyebrow raised in speculation. "Someone like you. You are so friendly and candid. Surely he isn't distant with you."

He would have laughed if her tone and the intent set to her mouth were less serious. "I'm just a lowly sergeant. Besides, most of my dealings with the general have been for disciplinary reasons. I wasn't the ideal trooper when I first joined."

A smile reached into her eyes. "Do tell."

"Let's just say I had a difficult time adjusting to army life. As much as I wanted to conform, I rebelled hard and often to the strictness. Finally, after several stints in the disciplinary barracks, I learned how to fit in."

"Not so easy when you think and feel differently than the others around you."

She didn't begin to know the half of it. He unfurled an arm and tapped the tip of her nose with his finger. "What do you know about being different than others?"

"I know more than you think. While my aunt and uncle were kind enough, I never felt as if I belonged at Meadowdale." She heaved a sigh. "Why didn't Father send for me before the fiasco with Sam? Am I that unlovable?"

Her wounded tone sliced into his heart. "Little lady, you are quite lovable. So lovable in fact, that I'm having a difficult time fighting the urge to pull you into my arms."

"Then don't."

"Don't what?"

"Don't fight it. Take me into your arms. Kiss me like you did in the doorway, only deeper and longer."

****

His intense gaze traveled over her face as if searching for an answer. He lifted a hand and stroked a knuckle along her cheek. Heat blossomed in its path. She briefly closed her eyes and savored the pleasant sensation.

"You are so beautiful. A man could lose himself in you."

She opened her eyes and fell into pools of liquid gold. A breath hitched in her throat. He could melt ice with that gaze.

"Let's get lost together," she whispered.

The tautness around his mouth eased. He lowered his head and pressed his lips to hers. Softly, gently, a chaste kiss of reverence. She wanted more. Much more.

She angled her mouth and drank of him. He tasted of whiskey. Had he fortified himself with a drink before coming upstairs? Because of her? Because of the strain she placed on him? He was a good man. The last thing she wanted was to be the cause of him descending into a bottle.

His lips started to retreat. She reached up and cupped his head, pulling him back. *Not yet, my sweet. We have only just begun.*

She let her fingers play in the soft curls and massage the tendons at the back of his neck. A groan rumbled from this throat. He shifted and leaned in, deepening their kiss. His tongue laved her lips and delved inside. Heat coiled in her lower belly. She moaned. This was the toe-curling kiss Christina had gone on and on about.

Emboldened, she let her tongue join his dance. Dip. Sway. Separate. Meld. Her blood heated. Her flesh tingled. She arched her hips. She wanted to feel him pressed against her, wanted his hands finding those special places that cried out for his touch. Nothing else mattered except the pleasing sensations growing inside her.

A flash of lightning lit the room, followed by a

boom of thunder that rattled the window. She couldn't stop a gasp. Gabe pulled away, taking his heat with him. A deep frown creased his brow.

She gently tugged on his arm. "It's just a storm. Come back to me. My lips are growing cold."

He wriggled out of her grasp and rolled away. "We can't do this, Meg."

"Why not?" Thoughts surfaced of another woman being entitled to his heart and body. He had never mentioned being affianced. But that didn't mean he wasn't. Jealousy flared inside her. "Is there someone else? Are you committed to another?"

"There is no one else."

Her heart fell. "Then it's me. You don't care enough to share yourself with me."

He scooped up her hand and brought it to his lips. "My caring for you is the reason I'm stopping this. You are dealing with a great many issues right now. Finding Orion. Moving to a strange place. Meeting your father for the first time in years. You don't need me adding any complications."

"You are not a complication, Gabe. You are my lifesaver, my friend, and more if you want it."

His gaze filled with dark clouds. He slipped off the bed and pushed to his feet. He turned and faced her, his expression wan. "As much as I want more, I'm not the man for you. There are things about me you wouldn't begin to understand."

"What kind of things?"

Another flash exploded in the window, followed immediately by a long roll of thunder that shook the walls and the bed. She shuddered. Storms had never bothered her before, but this one seemed exceptionally fierce. It matched the tempest Gabe appeared to be struggling with. He stood there, broiling in his own emotions. It showed in the deep lines etched on his face and in the defeated slump to his shoulders.

"Please tell me, Gabe. I would never judge you. You know that."

"You might believe you wouldn't, but once you learn of what I—"

A knocking on the door drummed into the room, cutting off his words. His gaze raced to the door and then returned. He set a finger to his lips and whispered, "Stay there and keep quiet."

She nodded and pulled the coverlet up to her chin. Her heart thudded. Nothing good ever came from an early morning caller.

He padded to the pallet and scooped his pistol off the floor. He then faced the door, weapon at the ready. "Who is it?"

"'Tis Mick McCormick from downstairs. I have information on Sloan for you."

Gabe threw the lock and opened the door. Lamplight spilled in from the hallway. She could just make out the burly bartender standing in the doorway still wearing his white and blue striped apron.

"My apologies for interrupting your sleep, Sergeant, but I have learned of news regarding Nate Sloan and his bunch. Since I take to my bed for most of the day after a long night tending bar, I figured you might want to be hearing it sooner rather than later."

Gabe lowered his pistol. "There's no need to apologize. We will gladly accept information on Sloan at any time of the day or night. What have you heard?"

"I have a man who helps me clean after the bar

closes for the night. I told himself about you folks and that you were looking for Sloan and his thugs. He said he saw a group of rough-looking men ride through late the night before. Could have been Sloan's gang, but he wasn't sure."

Her heart skipped a beat. It had to be the thieves. It had to be. "Ask him about Orion," she blurted.

Gabe shifted but did not turn her way. "Did your man mention seeing any of the men riding a black stallion?"

"That he did. Said one of them rode a fine-looking stallion with a coat black as coal."

Praise the Lord. Her prayers had been answered. She clamped down on the urge to bounce out of the bed and dance a jig. "Did your friend say how the stallion appeared? Had he been mistreated in any way?"

Over Gabe's shoulder, she could make out the bartender shucking off his cap and wagging his head. "No, Miss. Ben didn't say anything particularly specific. Just that all the horses were lathered and a wee bit droopy headed. Even the riders looked done in."

Gabe nodded. "That's because those men had been riding hard to escape justice. They robbed the Santa Fe back in Augusta. Took a payroll and that black stallion which belongs to us."

Us. She quite liked the sound of that. As if they were a family.

"Ben knew they were trouble the minute they rode in," the bartender added. "He said they were heavily armed and set out sentries while the others took care of watering the horses."

That they took time to water their mounts gave her hope. Perhaps the robbers had at least a thimble full of compassion. It might just be enough to keep Orion alive.

"Did your man Ben overhear them say anything about where they were headed?" Gabe asked.

She cocked an ear and leaned closer. She didn't want to miss a word of the bartender's answer.

"Some of the men were grumbling about needing to sleep. The leader said they could rest once they reached their safehouse."

"Any idea where that might be?"

"Wish I did. Then the law could put those men behind bars where they belong. Ben did mention that one of the men spoke about seeing his Border Queen señorita. Maybe this safehouse is somewhere near there?"

A possible lead. That was the best news she'd had in days. She couldn't keep the giddiness out of her voice. "Are you familiar with this place, Gabe? Is it close?"

Gabe turned his head. His expression was anything but happy. "If it's the same place I'm thinking of, then I know it. The Border Queen, also known as Caldwell, is a cow town sitting on the border between Kansas and the Oklahoma territories. It's about a day's ride from here."

"That's wonderful news."

He grunted. "Perhaps."

"Why do you say it like that?"

"Caldwell is a rough town, especially this time of year. It's a place to be avoided at all costs. I wouldn't go there unless I absolutely had to."

Her excitement took a chilling dip. "But we will go there. We have to."

Gabe didn't answer. He merely bent and fished some bills from his saddlebag. He handed them to the bartender. "Thank you for bringing us information on the riders, Mr. McCormick. See that your friend Ben gets a share for his help."

McCormick snuggled on his cap. "I will. Thank you, Sergeant. And if you and your sister are thinking of going after them hooligans…be mighty careful."

Chapter Nine

The soft clop of hooves and the creak of saddle leather were the only sounds breaking the monotonous quiet. Gabe rode ahead of her on the path, his mount moving smoothly as butter over hot bread. Unlike her mount. They had used more of their precious funds to purchase a horse for her to ride...if one could call the thing a horse. It had a deep swayback and a choppy, jarring gait. If she made it to the next stopping point without her bones disintegrating, it would be a miracle.

Sunlight dribbled through the leafy canopy and sparkled on the pond lapping at the edge of the pathway. Her throat was raw. Her bottom ached from sitting in the saddle for so long. A cool drink or even a quick dip sounded wonderful. But such indulgences might cause them to miss Sloan. The thieves had a two-day lead on them and could head for another safehouse at any moment.

She fingered the leather reins, needing a place to channel her restlessness. How was Orion faring? While the fleeing robbers had stopped in Lasley to water their mounts, Sloan refused to let them rest. Such a punishing pace could lead to injuries or worse. Her earlier hope of finding him unharmed was fading fast.

Gabe must have sensed her distress. He reined his horse to a stop and dismounted. "It's past midday. This thicket looks like a good place to rest and let the horses get a drink. We can have something to eat as well. After skipping breakfast, I'm famished."

A slight tug on the reins was all the encouragement her mount needed to halt. Her body sighed at the cessation of the jolting movement. She couldn't stop her shoulders from slumping. "We can rest and water the horses, but I'm not hungry."

He closed the distance between them in three quick strides. "You have to eat, Meg. If only to preserve your strength."

"I'm too twisted inside to eat." Not to mention her stomach had surely been jostled out of place by her mount's pitching gait.

"You must keep up your health, Meg. If you don't, you risk falling ill. That will put a halt to our journey while you recuperate, and make finding Orion all the harder."

Why did he always have to be right? If she wasn't so tired, she would scream. All she could do was nod. "Very well."

He held up his hands, and she leaned over and slid from the saddle. Every muscle in her body shrieked in protest. Her knees buckled, and she slumped against him. His arms wrapped around her, warm and steadying. She could stay like this forever. But that would show weakness. She didn't want to give him any reason to turn back.

She braced herself and pushed away. "You can let go now. I'm fine."

"Are you sure?"

"Yes. Go and water the horses. They need your attention more than I do."

His supportive arms left her waist. She wobbled a

bit but managed to stay upright. She could do this. She had to.

Gabe opened his mouth to say more but turned without uttering a word and crossed to his horse. He untied the blanket roll from the back of his saddle and returned.

He unfurled the blanket onto the ground at the edge of the pond. "There. That will provide some cushioning from the hard ground. Sit and rest. I'll be back with the food McCormick packed for us once I see to the horses."

Did he think she needed cushioning because she was weak, or was he just being a gentleman? Best to not take any chances. She waited for him to turn his back and then slowly lowered herself onto the blanket. Every muscle in her body wept. She closed her eyes, willing the pain to recede.

After a few minutes and with the help of a warm shaft of sunlight, her aches settled to a mild whining. She opened her eyes. Once they returned to civilization, she would indulge in a long, lavender-infused bath. Not only would she smell nice, her muscles would thank her.

She watched as Gabe tended to the horses. He was so efficient. Not one wasted movement. Or wasted thought either. His mind moved two steps ahead of everything he did or said. It had taken all her debating skills to convince him to modify their journey to include a stop in Caldwell. They had nothing to lose by trying, she had argued.

He fought a gallant fight, but he was no match for her tenacity. He eventually conceded, although not without caveats. She was to obey his every order without question. And she could not go off on her own for any reason. Those were things she could live with...she grunted under her breath...unless a dire situation dictated otherwise.

Gabe returned with his saddlebag in tow. He dropped onto the blanket beside her and began setting out their food. Sliced cheese and bread and strips of dried meat. Pemmican, Mr. McCormick had called it. Developed by the Indians for sustenance when traveling long distances. She was willing to try it. So was her stomach. It must have righted itself as it rumbled quite loudly.

If Gabe heard the hungry grumbling, he didn't comment on it. He merely held out a canteen. "Would you like some water? It's fresh. I just filled it from the pond."

She nodded and took the canteen. She lifted it to her lips and treated herself to a long, soothing drink. Cool water bathed her raw throat. She couldn't contain a moan.

"I apologize for pushing you so hard. I should have realized you weren't accustomed to riding for such long periods of time."

She shook her head and handed him the canteen. "Don't apologize. It's what I wanted. I'll be fine once we get to Caldwell."

He capped the canteen and pointed to the blanket. "Have something to eat. It's not much, but it will sate your hunger and provide some nourishment."

She set a slice of cheese on a piece of bread and popped it into her mouth. Simple, but delicious. And just what she needed.

They lapsed into silence while they ate. A breeze

whistled in the treetops. Birds sang from the branches. It was the perfect place for a picnic. Peaceful and relaxing. There was no telling when she might have a chance to indulge in such an amusement once she reached Fort Dent. The garrison and the man who commanded it were enigmas. For that matter, so was the man taking her there.

She braced her arms behind her and studied him from beneath half-closed eyelids. The tension around his mouth had eased. Even his brow held fewer furrows than usual. Perhaps he was relaxed enough to talk openly, to unveil the mystery surrounding him.

"Earlier, you said there were things about you that I wouldn't understand. What did you mean?"

He froze, the tautness returning to his lips. "Are you done?"

"Pardon?"

"Are you finished eating?"

At her nod, he busied himself with packing away the uneaten food in quick, jerky movements. She sighed. Not relaxed enough, it appeared.

He closed the saddlebag flap and sat back. "I'm not avoiding your question, Meg. It's just that there is more to me than most people know. Some can accept it. Most cannot."

What in the world kind of secret did he hold? She leaned forward, intrigued. "As you must have discovered during our short time together, I am not most people."

He let go a chuckle. "That you are not."

"Then tell me. Let me be the judge of what I can and cannot accept."

Fingers fidgeted with a wrinkle in the blanket. His

expression was just as twitchy, flickering from worried to sad to ill-at-ease. He drew in a breath and let it go on a long exhale. "There are things in my past I'm not proud of."

"Like not being the ideal soldier?"

"That's part of it."

She waited for more. A leaf tumbled across the blanket. A bird dove from one branch to another. Lunch pitched in her stomach. He didn't have faith in her judgment. That hurt more than a slap to the face.

She swallowed around the lump clogging her throat. "You said you care for me. Were those just empty words?"

He reached over and gathered her hand in his. "I do care for you. More than you know. But I'm not sure there can be a future for us. Your father may not approve of me. He could refuse to grant me permission to see you."

Anger overrode her hurt. "My father gave up his right to have any say in my life long ago. The only reason I agreed to go live with him was to save my aunt and uncle from the pettiness of others."

"You may think he doesn't have any power over you, but as my commander, he can make things very difficult for us. He could send me on endless patrols. Post me to evening and night sentry duty. He could even have me transferred to another post."

"I would go with you."

He wagged his head. "Knowing General Myer, it would be a rough post with few amenities and fewer decent women. You would be miserable."

"Not any more miserable than living with a father who thinks he can control my life...our lives." At his desolate expression, she cupped his cheek with her hand. "We can deal with him later when all of this is over. Right now, let's just focus on what we do have."

He turned his head slightly and pressed a kiss into her palm. "And what *do* we have?"

She leaned forward and brushed her lips to his. "Each other."

He slid his hand to the back of her neck and pulled her closer. His lips pressed against hers, gently at first, then deeper as if searching for something more. What more, she wasn't quite certain. But she was sure it would be most pleasurable.

Her aches ebbed. Her troubled thoughts subsided. There was no overwhelming rush to be someplace else. It was just the here and now.

Their lips mated. Tongues danced. The space around them evaporated until it was just the two of them with their shallow breaths melded into one. His fingers caressed the back of her neck, sending shivers coursing through her. If this was heaven, she never wanted to leave.

A blackbird's crow spilled down from the treetops, raucous and loud, and bursting the moment like a fragile soap bubble.

Gabe pulled away and glanced skyward. A frown returned to his face. "As much as I want to keep kissing you, we should be going. I want to get settled in a hotel in Caldwell before night falls."

Caldwell. Sloan. Orion. Rescuing her beloved stallion should be at the forefront of her thoughts. Her needs, her desires, would have to wait.

****

The whiskey was good. The cards even better.

Thanks to a bit of sly manipulation. The angel sitting on his shoulder wagged its head. He'd used his gift before at cards, and it had turned deadly. He brushed the cherub away. He would be cautious this time. No overplaying his hand. No anger. No reprisals. This was for Orion. For Meg.

She was safely ensconced in the Caldwell Hotel just down the street, and hopefully fast asleep. She didn't need to be out in the lawless town where gunfights and hangings were commonplace. He had to keep her safe. From the bad elements and from himself. What happened in the Lasley hotel room and in the seclusion of the thicket could go no further. Not until he had her father's blessing for marriage…which may never be given.

"You gonna play or stare at them cards all night?"

Cripes. Caught woolgathering. He'd best get his mind on his task or he risked a bullet to the head.

He shucked two cards from his hand and placed them face down on the table. "My apologies, gentlemen. I'm feeling the long ride from Fort Smith. I'll take two."

The dealer, a wisecracker named Bob who owned a general store just down the street, shifted his cigar from one side of his mouth to the other with only his teeth and tongue. Impressive. He'd tried to do that before and ended up with a lap full of lit cigar.

Bob dispensed two cards from the top of the deck and spoke around the stogie. "Not a problem, Sergeant. We'll be happy to keep taking your money."

He responded with a gullible smile. If the foursome gathered at the table knew he was purposefully letting them win, they would run him out under a hail of gunfire. Gamblers had their standards. No cheating, for any reason.

The odor of whiskey, old sweat, and cigar smoke swirled around the brightly lit room. It was the smell of his childhood, before Seaton House, before his and Sally's rescue from a brutal guardian. Memories surfaced of drunken rants, of painful punches, and most hurtful of all, blistering stabs of a lit cigar. He still carried the scars, scattered on his body like grisly tattoos. He drew in a calming breath. No one would have that much power over him again. Ever.

He shifted in his chair and took a quick survey of the room. Nearly every table was full of drinkers and card players. A busy Saturday night for the Red Rose Saloon, a favorite watering hole of the townsfolk *and* delinquents on the run. So far, there had been no sign of Sloan or his men. An earlier visit with the Caldwell sheriff confirmed that no one had seen the bunch in months. He'd just have to use his wiles to find out if and where the thieves might be holed up.

He pushed a five-spot into the kitty. He had a decent hand. A pair of jacks, a four, a queen, and an ace. No "wild cards" for this group of regulars. Just plain draw poker.

Old Joe ran the livery at the end of the street where they had stabled their horses after arriving in town. The stable owner had invited him to join their group at the Red Rose when he inquired about a place to get a drink and play a hand or two of cards. The best places to uncover information were saloons and bordellos. Men's tongues slackened with the entertainment found in both.

Joe wagged his head and folded. "That's it for me."

"Me as well," Bob grunted.

That left him and Harper. Perfect. That's where the goods were, and he needed to do some marketing. Sheriff Brown had told him if Sloan was hiding nearby, Clive Harper would be the one to question.

Clive had elected to take no cards. Either he was bluffing, or he had been dealt a respectable hand. Not that it mattered. An ace up the sleeve would ensure the man came up lacking. He'd used his gift earlier to secret the card away until he needed it most. And that time was now. All he needed was a distraction. Nothing dramatic. Just a little something to draw Clive's attention. His earlier thoughts triggered an idea.

He gathered energy in his head. His temples pulsed. His skull swirled with warmth. He focused on the dealer. *Sorry, Bob, but I need your help.*

He gave a little push. Just enough to…yes, that's it. Smoldering ashes from the tip of Bob's cigar broke off and dropped onto the man's lap. Bob hollered and shoved upright with his stogie still clamped in his teeth.

Joe grabbed a glass and tossed whiskey at Bob's smoking pants. Blue flames erupted and fanned out. The dealer bellowed and began hopping up and down and slapping at his crotch. A little more drama than he needed, but he would take it.

He glanced at Harper. The man's attention was squarely focused on Bob. Good. It was time to spring his trap *and* get his money back. Using a quick, furtive movement, he traded the queen in his hand for the ace tucked in his sleeve. There was no need for overkill. He just needed to win.

Bob finally subdued the fire and settled back onto his chair. He stubbed his cigar in an ashtray with a disgusted grunt. "All right, gentlemen, let's finish this while I still have most of my pants left. Clive, I believe it's your play."

Harper's lips curled into a smile. Not a laughing one. A self-satisfied one. A tell if he ever saw one. But that smugness wouldn't last long.

"I call," Harper said as he laid down his cards face-up.

Two pair, threes and tens. Usually a winning hand. Not this time.

Gabe fanned out his cards on the table. Jacks and aces beat threes and tens any day of the week. Red climbed in Harper's face. His jaw muscle twitched as if he chewed on something tough. Bon appétit.

Gabe grinned and shoveled the kitty toward himself. "Looks like my luck has finally changed, gentlemen."

Harper grabbed his whiskey and downed the entire glass. Perfect. Have another and another. Secrets tended to spill over drink-loosened tongues.

Harper's bankroll had dwindled to a few coins and a lone bill. He pointed to the pile. "Do you need me to spot you any, Clive?"

"Nah. Johnson will stake me." Harper pushed upright. "He knows I'm good for it."

He'd met John Johnson earlier at the bar when the man served him a whiskey. Chatty fellow. Knew most of the regulars. If Harper wasn't going to give up the goods on Sloan, perhaps the bartender would. That would be his next stop if Harper didn't pan out.

Shouts and pounding hooves cascaded through the open doorway and into the bar. A shot rang out and then another. He tensed and grabbed the edge of the table, ready to duck underneath should the shooters come inside.

Jim wagged his head. "No need to get jumpy, Sergeant. That's just the cowhands from the Dewitt ranch letting off a little steam. They're heading over to the Honeypot for some Saturday night recreation."

The commotion faded just as quickly as it broiled up. He rolled the tension out of his shoulders and nodded. "Sounds like my troopers after a long patrol. Dusty and tired, but eager to enjoy a night of women and whiskey."

"Yep. Some mighty pretty gals over there at the Honeypot. You might give it a go after our game."

He doubted Meg would appreciate him frequenting such a place. She had bristled like an agitated porcupine at his announcement of visiting the Red Rose. Hopefully he would find all the information he needed right here. Going to the Honeypot would be his last resort. If he was honest with himself, he just wasn't interested in other women. A blonde-haired, blue-eyed lady held his attention.

Harper returned to the table with a fresh bankroll and a bottle of whiskey. He poured himself a drink and passed the bottle around.

Gabe tipped his glass. "Thanks for the drink, Clive. Are we celebrating anything in particular?" Like the arrival of Nate Sloan and a stolen payroll?

"Just feeling generous is all."

Generous he could handle...provided it came in the form of the information he sought. He set his drink on the table and began shuffling the cards. "You mentioned your spread earlier, Clive. Are you running any cattle out there? From what I've seen, beef cows appear to be the staple around these parts."

Harper took a sip of whiskey. "I have a dozen or so black Angus. Pigs are what keep me afloat. Got ten sows that pop out nearly a dozen piglets at each farrowing. Easy money."

"Whew." He wrinkled his nose. "Reckon you don't have many visitors what with all the noise and smell."

"The smell's not so bad. You get used to it after a while."

"Moonshine helps bring in the visitors," Bob said. "Clive makes the best corn likker in these parts. He built a soddy in the side of a hill big enough to hold his corn supply, a copper still, and a parlor for drinking. With fresh creek water running nearby, it's the perfect place for a stillhouse."

And the perfect place to hide criminals on the run. He'd bet his last dollar that's where Sloan and his men were holed up.

He began dealing the cards. "I sure could use some good corn liquor to take back with me to Fort Smith. Any chance I could ride out tomorrow and see this fancy still house of yours and get a jug?"

Harper's jaw muscle jerked like a fish tossed onto a creek bank. He wagged his head. "Wish I could accommodate you, Sergeant, but I don't have any liquor in stock right now."

"What?" Bob said. "You said you siphoned off a batch last week. You couldn't have sold out that quickly. What happened to it?"

"It was a bad batch. I had to throw it out."

Bob grunted. "Well, that was a damn waste."

"It sure was. But it couldn't be helped. Maybe you can come out and visit the next time you ride through, Sergeant."

The man tried to look consoling but failed. Miserably. His eyes shifted way too much for contriteness. Gabe's skin tingled. There was more to Harper's simple explanation. Much more. He knew it in his bones. Come first light, he would take his suspicions to Sheriff Brown and hopefully convince the lawman to investigate.

Chapter Ten

Meg reined her horse to a stop behind the men dismounting near a small grove of cottonwood trees and hedges tucked between two hillocks. Golden halos of morning sunlight gilded the treetops. It was the sign of angels. The sign of hope. She needed hope. A lot of it.

Worry over Orion ate at her insides. She wanted to be there when they freed him from the thieves. Had to be there. She wanted him to see a familiar, caring face. Wanted to ensure if he had sustained any injuries that he got immediate treatment. The livery owner had supplied them with various medical supplies for treating injured horses. Gabe's saddlebag bulged with the man's generosity. It appeared Gabe's late-night adventure at the Red Rose Saloon had been fruitful in more ways than one.

He had come to her room at dawn to report his findings and his winnings. He had added to their funds, instead of depleting them as she had feared. While she cheered his cleverness, a part of her wondered if there was more to his account of the night. Like a romp with one of the painted ladies?

All night long, she had listened for his return. Hour after agonizing hour. Finally, in the wee hours of the morning, the rasp of a key and the squawk of door hinges rang out from the hotel room next to hers. Soft thuds filtered through the wall and then there was silence. If he had brought anyone else with him, their tryst had been awful quiet.

She gave herself a mental shake. Why did she allow her thoughts to sink into fetid bogs? Gabe was good and honest. He wouldn't trifle with her affections like that. Besides, he had agreed without any argument to let her join the posse riding to Clive Harper's farm. He must have sensed her desperate need to be included, regardless of whether the thieves were there or not.

Of course, she was to remain secluded in a safe spot, far from any skirmish that might erupt. An acceptable mandate. She had no desire to be anywhere near a gun battle. The shooting in the Lasley Hotel had been more than enough exposure to violence.

Like bees in a hive, the group of lawmen went quickly and quietly about their business, seeing to their horses and readying their weapons. After hearing Gabe's suspicions about Sloan's whereabouts, Sheriff Brown had assembled a five-man posse to investigate. She prayed they found the thugs, and that no one was hurt during the encounter. Most especially not…

A blue army slouch hat bobbed over the other heads. *Gabe.* He had come to mean more to her than she ever imagined. For the first time in her life, she looked forward to the future instead of dreading it. If anything happened to him…No. She wouldn't think that way. Everything would turn out just fine. She would have Orion back, and everyone, including Gabe, would be safe.

He threaded his way through the lawmen and headed toward her. Her heart sprang like a jackrabbit in springtime, just as it always did when he was near. Her feelings for him were different than for Teddy. She enjoyed being around Gabe and wanted to spend every moment with him. Like last night. She felt adrift and very much alone while he was out gathering information. Not so with Teddy. When his visits ended, she had breathed a sigh of relief.

Gabe stopped beside her horse and held out his hands. "This is as far as you go, Little Sister."

Hmmph. That brotherly tone would change once this mission was over and they were back in the privacy of a hotel room. Her lips tingled at the thought of his delicious kisses. She would never tire of tasting him.

"Meg?"

She doused her errant thoughts and slid from the saddle. It was a good thing he couldn't read minds. He needed to focus on the mission ahead with no distractions.

He set her on the ground and dropped his hands to his sides. "We'll secure the horses to a picket line in this thicket and walk the rest of the way. You will stay here and wait for us to return."

She shaded her eyes with a hand and peered across the vast stretch of rolling hills. "How far away is this soddy house?"

Gabe motioned to a tall hillock rising to the south. "If Harper's still is where Sheriff Brown believes it to be, then just over that ridge. About half a mile. We'll surround the place and launch an attack. Since it's still early, hopefully we'll catch the thugs off guard."

The word *attack* ricocheted in her head. Bullets and blood. Chaos and confusion. Just like in Lasley. Her insides turned to ice. She rested a hand on his arm, needing an anchor for her fears. "Please be careful, Gabe."

"Don't worry. If Sloan is there, we'll get Orion back safe and sound."

"I meant for yourself."

His eyes softened. "I'm not going anywhere. I have something to look forward to after all this is over."

Her blood warmed. She managed a smile. "So do I."

The clearing of a throat doused the flames spreading between them. She pulled her hand away and pasted on her most benign expression, one a sister might wear for her brother. She would play along with Gabe's game…for now.

Sheriff Brown tipped his hat. "Sorry to interrupt, Miss, but I wanted to discuss our plan of attack with the sergeant. Make sure we cover every contingency."

"There's no need to apologize. We all want this operation to go as smoothly and safely as possible." She leaned over and snagged her mount's reins. "I'll see to my horse and leave you to your plans."

She led the horse deeper into the thicket, their footfalls softened by a carpet of deadfall. Midway inside, half a dozen horses stood secured to a rope stretched between two stout trees. That must be the *picket line* Gabe had mentioned. Odd name for it. She would ask him about the origin of the term once this was all over. She prayed that would be soon and without bloodshed. As he said, they had so much to look forward to.

She guided her horse into the open spot beside Gabe's mount and looped the reins around the rope. She tied a secure knot and then sidestepped to the horse's middle. She loosened the saddle girth so the animal could breathe easier during the wait. She could only hope Orion had been treated as compassionately.

A few feet from the picket line, a downed tree rested on the ground. It would be a good spot to sit and watch over the horses. There was no telling how long this operation might take. It could be hours. Best to make herself comfortable.

She crossed to the log and pressed on the wood. The bark remained firm and securely attached. Not rotted yet. Good. She wouldn't be dumped unceremoniously on her derriere. It had happened once before at Meadowdale. She and Sam had laughed about her up-ending for hours. This was not the time for hilarity.

She settled on the log and glanced around. Tall cottonwood and pockets of brush dotted the thicket. Steam rose from the trunks where the sun's rays touched. The only sounds breaking the quiet were the occasional snort of a horse and the soft drone of conversation drifting from the other side of the thicket.

Gabe and the other lawmen stood listening to the sheriff. Some nodded; others, like Gabe, absorbed their instructions without reaction. After a few minutes, the talking stopped. Gabe turned in her direction and gave a quick wave. As much as she would prefer a sweet, departing kiss, she would take the simple gesture.

He joined the lawmen slogging up the short incline. They quickly crested the hillock and disappeared over the other side like wraiths into the mist. Her finger found and fidgeted with a loose piece of bark. If the fiasco of Orion's abduction was soon to be over, what awaited her at Fort Dent? Would her father accept Gabe in her life? If not, could he make Gabe's life miserable as he had warned? She snapped the bark free with a flick of her finger. Her father couldn't be that hard-hearted. He just couldn't.

What little she could remember of him had been happy. Strolls in the park with Mama holding one of her hands and Father the other. One time, he had bought them cream icies from a hokey-pokey vendor. A most delicious treat.

His eyes were blue, like hers. And he had a long beard that tickled her face when she snuggled against him. Why had he given all that up? Did she no longer matter to him after Mama's death? Had she ever mattered to him?

Tears welled in her eyes. Breathing became a chore. She pushed to her feet and stalked to the picket line. No matter what she found at Fort Dent, she wouldn't let it stop her from having what mattered to her now…a future with Gabe.

She stopped in front of her mount and rubbed its ears. The gelding lowered its head and sniffed the apples she'd stored in her pocket for Orion. The horse gave a gentle snort and nudged her hip.

"So you have a sweet tooth, too, do you?"

It nudged her again. She scratched a hairy ear. She could spare a slice for this sweet animal. She just needed a knife. She glanced at the leather bag attached to Gabe's saddle. The livery owner had included a long, slender knife as part of the necessary medical supplies. That would do perfectly.

She ducked under the picket line and eased between her mount and Gabe's. She flipped up the pouch lid and fished inside. There was a small jar, a pair of gloves, linen strips, twine, and…something unexpected. Something wrapped in oilskin. That wasn't part of the supplies. It was the size of a folded letter. A personal item of Gabe's? She shouldn't go through his belongings, but curiosity got the better of her.

She withdrew the oilskin and unfurled the folds. It was a letter, creased and faded with age. She gently pried open the letter. The handwriting was shaky and faded but still readable.

My dearest Gabriel,

I don't know how much longer I have in this world, so I'm writing to tell you how very proud I am of the wonderful young man you have become, even at such a tender age. You are full of courage and kindness. For you, family comes above all else. I have no doubts that after I am gone, you will see that Sally is loved and well cared for. Stay safe and remember to use your gift wisely.

Love always, Mother.

Tears welled in her eyes. His mother thought he was gifted. Didn't all mothers think that of their sons and daughters? She knew if she were ever blessed with children of her own, she would think the same.

She gently folded the oilskin back over the letter. Gabe clearly treasured this memento of his mother. How lucky of him. The only thing her mother had left her was emptiness.

The distant bark of gunfire rifled into her gloomy thoughts. Her pulse jumped. So did the horses. She quickly stuffed the oilskin back in the saddle pouch and ducked under the picket line. Heart thudding, she crossed to the edge of the grove and rushed up the slope. At the crest, she went down on her knees and stared across the rolling landscape at the southern hillock. Other than the sporadic gunfire, nothing disturbed the peaceful serenity.

Minutes passed. Or was it hours? The gunfire slowed and then stopped. She clutched a hand over her heart. Was it over? Was anyone hurt?

****

A tense silence fell over the clearing. Lying prone on the hard ground, Gabe went up on his elbows for a quick look. Nothing moved in or around the soddy house. Just a thick cloud of smoke swirled over the ground. He grunted and rolled onto his back. Only a fool would be taken in by the lull. A very dead fool.

He emptied the spent casings and loaded in fresh ammunition. This skirmish was not over. Not by a long shot. Sloan had refused to surrender when Sheriff Brown hailed him and advised that the house was surrounded and that they should come out with their hands up. The thugs had answered the demand with gunfire. There was no doubt in his mind that Sloan and his cronies were regrouping and preparing for another fight.

A chill rattled through him. The cool morning dew had soaked through his shirt and dampened his skin. He ignored the discomfort. Better to be alive on top of the earth than dead and buried six feet under it.

He turned onto his side and signaled his intent to approach the north side of the soddy. Lying a few feet away, Sheriff Brown nodded and pointed to the south. A smart fox, the lawman. He'd planned the attack down to the last detail. The wild West could use more men like him.

Gabe rolled into a crouch and paused, muscles tensing. All remained quiet and still. Good. He was brave, but not that brave. Running through a hail of bullets was not his idea of fun.

He glanced at the sheriff. Not a pucker of hesitation showed on the lawman's face. A tough hombre, that one. Brown gave a nod, and they took off at a fast trot, him going north and the lawman to the south. No gunfire greeted their charge. He reached the house and pasted his back against the earthen wall. The only sound breaking the silence was the quick draws of his own breaths. Had the posse's volley immobilized the thugs? Numerous holes peppered the sod, a solid barricade, but not solid enough to stop a bullet.

A noise shuffled into the quiet. Fifty yards from the soddy, a handful of horses milled about a small corral, their movements stirring up clouds of dust. A shiny black coat shimmered among the browns. Orion. The stallion appeared to be unharmed. A bit unnerved by the gunfire, but unscathed.

One question answered. He turned his attention back to the soddy house. A more dangerous matter to solve.

He inched toward the closed door. Sheriff Brown did the same. They stopped just shy of the jamb on each side. There was still no sound or movement coming from inside. Were the thugs dead or just playing possum? Only one way to find out.

He pointed to the door and then to himself. Sheriff Brown nodded, his expression calm as standing water. Gabe sucked in a breath and rolled in front of the door. It appeared to be flimsy enough. He hefted his leg and gave a hearty kick. The door careened open. He rushed inside, gun at the ready. The sheriff surged in behind him.

There was no countering gunfire. No shouts or

movement. The small room was quiet as a funeral parlor. A quick scan revealed two lifeless bodies sprawled to the left and two more to the right. There was no one else inside.

The sheriff toed one of the bodies onto its back. Pale eyes stared skyward. Gabe lowered his pistol. "Are any of them Sloan?"

The sheriff glanced at each of the bodies. "Nope. Sloan has dark eyes and black hair. None of these are him."

"Then where did he go?"

"Dunno. Maybe he got wind of our hunt for him and fled."

"I don't think so. The stallion he stole is still out in the corral along with the other mounts." Gabe pointed to several bulging burlap bags crowding the corner of the room. "I'll bet those contain the stolen payroll. He wouldn't have abandoned those unless he needed to leave in a hurry."

The sheriff holstered his pistol. "Maybe he slipped through our perimeter somehow."

A memory emerged of the fortress he had built in the woods near Seaton House. He'd dug an escape tunnel in case he needed to make a fast escape from imaginary villains. Perhaps Clive Harper had done the same with his still house. Set in the side of a hill, a tunnel would be an easy dig.

He turned in a circle, surveying the room. The only spot large enough to conceal a hole would be behind the copper still sitting in the back corner. He crossed the room in three quick strides and bent around the still. A gaping hole large enough for a man to crawl through glared back at him. Damn. Damn. Damn. The snake had slithered through their trap.

He straightened. "There's a tunnel over here, Sheriff. Looks like it heads to the west. I'll go in and see where it ends up. You and your men can return to the thicket and get the horses. Start scouting the area. Sloan couldn't have gone far on foot."

As the sheriff left the soddy house, Gabe holstered his pistol and eyed the tunnel. It was only wide enough to belly crawl through. Hopefully, he would make it to the end without the walls collapsing on him. Being buried alive was not the way he wanted his life to end.

Steeling himself with a deep slug of air, he dove into the hole and inched forward. The smell of dank earth and rot filled his nostrils. The deeper he went, the darker and damper the tunnel got. Clods of dirt began raining on his head. Panic welled inside him. He counted off the elbow thrusts propelling him forward. Not. Going. To. Die. Not. Today.

After what seemed like hours, a circle of gray loomed ahead. He pushed out a relieved breath. This tunnel would not become his grave.

As gray turned to white, he slowed and cocked an ear, listening for any sounds. The last thing he wanted was to emerge from the tunnel only to walk straight into an ambush.

All remained quiet. He continued the muscle-straining crawl until he reached the gaping exit. He stopped again and listened. Still nothing. He ducked his head out and back in. There was no reaction. So far, so good.

He unholstered his pistol and eased out of the hole. He crouched against the side of the hill where the tunnel ended. Footprints dotted the loose earth and headed toward a thicket of trees fifty yards away. Was Sloan holed up there, or had he continued his flight? By his estimate, the thug had about a half-hour head start on him.

He scaled the hill and scanned the surrounding area. There was no sign of the sheriff or his posse. The smart thing would be to fire a shot and alert the lawmen to his whereabouts. But that would also alert Sloan. He didn't want to give the miscreant any advantages with his escape. The man needed to pay for what he had done. He would just have to track Sloan on his own.

Saw grass slapped at his boots as he trotted across the short expanse. He made it to the shelter of one of the larger trees and pressed against the trunk. Only the wind sifting through the treetops broke the stillness. Good that he hadn't been fired at. Bad that he still didn't know where Sloan was.

He left the safety of the tree trunk and crept farther into the thicket, being careful where he placed his feet. The crack of a breaking twig could sound like a fourth of July firecracker in the quietness, even with the wind blowing.

Just ahead, a thick tangle of vines formed a man-sized hairball. A good place to bury into if one needed to hide. He inched forward. Nothing moved in or around the nest of vines. He crouched and cocked his head from side to side, trying to catch a glimpse of anything out of place in the greenery. Nothing jumped out at him. Just greens and browns and...

A whisper of sound tickled his ears. The hair on the back of his neck stood on end. Something or someone was in the thicket with him.

He dove to the ground and rolled. A gun barked,

and a bullet whizzed past his head. He flattened himself onto the carpet of leaves behind a skinny tree. Not nearly enough cover, but it would have to do.

A shadow darted through the trees to his left. Got you. He zeroed in on the target. Before he could pull the trigger, something solid pressed against his temple.

"Don't move," came a gruff voice.

Like hell. He spun away and kicked. The man went down with a grunt. Gabe raised his gun to shoot. A foot slapped the weapon from his hand. He tried to roll, but his attacker pounced on top of him. He grabbed hold of thick wrists, struggling to keep the man's pistol from lining up with his head. Black feral eyes drilled into him. *Sloan.*

The pistol barrel inched closer. His heart pounded. He didn't want to die. Not now. Not with a future with Meg waiting for him.

A metallic click sounded. Sloan was out of bullets. And about to get hammered with even more bad luck.

Gabe turned his head and locked eyes on his pistol half-buried under a pile of leaves. He gathered energy in his head. Heat swirled in his skull. He released one of Sloan's wrists and stretched out his arm. The gun flew across the ground and slapped into his palm.

Footfalls thudded toward them. He twisted and shot at the approaching attacker. The man dropped to the ground with a dull thud.

Something hard crashed into his cheek. Pain exploded in his mouth. He tasted blood and anger. Damn bastard. That was the second time Sloan had belted him with a gun. He recognized the man's voice the moment he spoke. He had been the robber who had cold-cocked him at the train.

He shook off the haze clouding his vision and shoved his pistol barrel under the thug's chin. "Keep still, Sloan. Or you're next."

The man ceased his movements. Gabe wriggled out from under him and pushed upright. He aimed his gun at the thief's head. "Drop your weapon. Slow and easy."

The pistol thudded to the ground. Sloan raised his hands in surrender. Dark eyebrows furrowed into one long line of bewilderment. "How'd you do that?"

He knew exactly what the man meant. But he wasn't going to respond. The bastard didn't deserve an answer.

Loud rustling blasted from the edge of the thicket. Sheriff Brown called out his name. Help had arrived. Not that he needed it. He had everything under control.

Chapter Eleven

"Tilt your head back and keep still. I promise to be gentle."

One skeptical eyebrow lifted. "You promise? I don't like pain. It hurts."

She dunked the cotton cloth in the basin of chilled water she'd placed on the table. Men. They could face a charging bear and not cringe. But let them require a little doctoring, and they turned into whimpering babies.

"Hush. That gash needs to be cleaned else it will fester. Now hold still."

When she first caught sight of Gabe's bloodied face, she had nearly fainted. But seeing him moving about in the glade with ease had allayed her fears. A closer inspection revealed a shallow, two-inch slash on his cheek. A gift from Sloan, he had told her. If the evil mongrel wasn't already heading for the hangman's noose, she would shoot him herself.

Gabe shifted on the chair but made no other carping quips. She squeezed out the excess water and then pulled the lamp closer to the edge of the table. Darkness had set in since their return to Caldwell, and she wanted to be able to see what she was doing.

She stepped in front of him and began gently pressing the wet cloth against the gash gouging his cheek. The bleeding had stopped, and the edges were starting to crust over. It didn't appear to need stitching. As long as no infection set in, the wound should heal just fine.

She smiled for the hundredth time since the raid had ended. All her prayers had been answered. Gabe was safe. So was Orion. The stallion had come out of the entire fiasco without a scratch. Although she'd almost strangled the horse with a fierce hug when they were reunited.

"Happy, are you?"

"Very happy. My world has been set back to right. I have Orion..." She dabbed at the bloody crust. "And I have you."

He winced. "Keep that up, and you might not have me for long."

Despite the joking tone, his words pinched. Her smile faded. Everyone she had ever loved left her. Her mother. Her father. Sam. Why would Gabe be any different?

"Hey." He gave her elbow a gentle squeeze. "You know that was said in jest."

She knew it was. But she couldn't stop the dark feelings from surfacing. Nothing good in her life ever lasted.

"I love you, Margaret Myer. You have me until the sun stops rising."

His words washed over her. He loved her. Only a handful of people had ever said that to her. Teddy, because it was required of him. Sam, because he was her best friend, and her mother. Different variations of love delivered for a variety of reasons. Yet, Gabe's vow was the sort of devotion that would last a lifetime. The sort of love she had always craved. Could she trust him with her heart?

Her throat tightened. She swallowed back a sob and busied herself with cleaning the last streaks of blood from his face.

"Well?"

She stilled her wiping and met a bewildered gaze. He wanted a response to his declaration of love. Guilt stabbed her. He deserved an answer after all he had done for her. But what to say? How to say it? Every reply sounded cold and disjointed. The last thing she wanted was to cause him pain.

She traded the bloodied cloth for a drying towel and wrapped her fingers in the soft cotton. Some confessions needed a good wringing to bring them to light.

"I'll admit I was intrigued by you from the moment we met."

He grunted, tawny eyes flashing with amusement. The imp. She ignored his teasing and continued. "Your honesty and integrity were refreshing after all I had been through. But I couldn't allow myself to fall for you. You are a soldier, the type of man my father would select for me to wed. I wasn't going to give him that satisfaction."

His expression turned sincere. "I can understand your hesitancy. You are your own woman. It's one of the things I love most about you."

He might understand, but her admission still cut. Pain flashed in his eyes for the briefest of seconds before he shuttered the emotion.

She patted the wet spots with the drying cloth. "After spending time with you, after discovering the real soldier behind the armor, I have learned that the satisfaction of being with you would be all mine. You are the best thing that has ever happened to me…besides Orion."

"You put me in the same category as a horse?"

"He is not just a horse. He is my life. And it's my fondest wish that you will be my life too."

"I hear a *but* in those words."

She traced a path along his jaw, drawing strength from the solidness. "I have been hurt in the past by those I love. I don't trust easily."

He grasped her hand and moved it to his chest, pressing her palm over his heart. "I swear on everything I treasure that I will never cause you harm. Ever. I would stab my own heart before hurting yours."

His earnestness plowed into her logjam of doubts. Leaks sprouted. In the short time they had been together, he had never tried to deceive her. Had never placed his own needs over hers. All he had ever wanted was for her to be happy and safe.

"You are a special man, Gabriel Hunt. Maybe too special for a tainted lady like me."

His eyebrows snapped together. "Hush that foolish talk. You are far from tainted. I'm lucky to even be allowed around your sunshine. I hope I can bask in your light for the rest of my life. If you'll have me, that is…"

The dam inside her broke apart. "My heart knows what it wants. I love you, Gabriel Hunt. From now until the sun stops shining."

He lifted her hand to his lips. "That's good. Because I aim to make you my wife."

Her pulse stuttered. "A-Are you asking me to marry you?"

"I am. I can't give you much, just a simple life

heaped with love and respect."

"That's all I need. All I ever wanted."

"Is that a yes?"

She let out a soft chuckle. "Yes, you buffoon. It's a yes. I will marry you."

"Good. My pouch of convincing ammunition was starting to run low." He frowned and glanced around the sparsely furnished room. "This is not exactly how I envisioned asking you to be my wife."

"How did you envision it?"

"Somewhere elegant with velvet-upholstered chairs and floors covered with thick wool carpeting. We would toast our engagement with champagne and enjoy a celebratory waltz on a marble dance floor."

"That sounds lovely. But it is not me. Not us. Our love was forged out on the rugged prairie. I think this plain hotel room with its faded wallpaper and creaky wood floor suits our engagement perfectly."

"You never fail to surprise me, Meg Myer. The simple things in life mean the most to you." He thumbed the yellow string circling her finger. "I noticed you always wear this. What is it for?"

"It's a reminder to learn from my mistakes and not make them again."

"Am I a mistake?"

"Oh, no. You are a gift. A very precious gift. I can only hope I don't ruin your goodness. I am not perfect."

"That's what your cousin Christina said when I came to collect you. She warned me not to fall under your spell. That you were anything but perfect."

A shadow fell over her newfound joy. "That sounds like Christina. For some reason, she resented my presence at Meadowdale. She found countless ways to vilify me in everyone's eyes, lying, trickery. No tactic was overlooked. She was the one who sent Teddy to the stables that day when he came calling. She knew I was there with Sam."

"Her insinuations fell on deaf ears, my love. You are as perfect a lady as any man could wish for." He pulled her onto his lap and wrapped her in a protective cocoon of arms. "And I am perfectly happy being under your spell."

Heat spread under her ribs. She wanted more of what that pleasing embrace promised. She eyed his lips. "I wonder…"

"Wonder what?"

"Would a kiss break the spell?"

"Let's see." He pressed a quick peck to her lips. "Nope. Still spellbound."

"Hmmph. You call that a kiss?" She wiggled in his lap, angling for a better approach to his lips.

He grabbed her by the hips, halting her movements. "Keep that up and this will be over before it begins."

Her pulse skipped a beat. "This what?"

"I think you know."

Oh, she did. Her body hummed with a desire to feel the things his kisses promised. But her head smoldered with misgivings. What if he found her lacking? Would he still want her?

He caressed her arm in soothing strokes. "We don't have to do anything you feel uncomfortable doing."

"I want to, very much so. I just don't…I don't know how…" Embarrassing heat climbed up her neck and spread into her ears. "Well, I lived on a farm, so I know the how. It's just…I'm not very well versed in…in the pleasing aspect."

He traced a path up her arm, over her shoulder, and onto her neck. Fingers dipped beneath her collar and toyed with her bare skin. "It would be my pleasure to teach you all you need to know."

****

Shadows cast by the lamplight danced on the walls. One shadow in particular held his attention. It had a head and arms that thrashed about. Faint thumps and the shush of fabric romped across the room. His pulse leapt at every sound. A March hare couldn't have been any jumpier.

The silhouette stilled, and quiet descended. Was she done? He hoped so. His eagerness wouldn't be contained much longer.

"You can turn around now."

He swallowed his last bit of moisture and swiveled on the chair seat. A breath lodged in his throat. Athena couldn't look more beautiful. He'd read about the Greek gods and goddesses in the books lining the library shelves at Seaton House. None of those Olympians held a candle to his Meg.

She sat on the edge of the bed, unclothed, her treasures bared for his eyes only. He had offered to help her undress, but she had declined. Said she wasn't quite prepared to undertake that lesson just yet. So he had turned his back, giving her privacy and the time needed to assemble her confidence.

Her skin glowed with milky silkiness. Hair of spun gold spilled over her shoulders and curled around her stomach. Rose-colored nipples peeked through the locks, teasing him with their pertness. A narrow waist sloped to generous thighs where a vee of darker curls pointed to the cave that awaited his plunder.

Heated blood surged inside him. He wanted her with a fierceness that burned. Against the wall. On the bed. Even on the chair would suffice. But he had to contain himself. Giving free rein to his desires would send any skittish filly running for the door. Her eyes were already round as saucers, and her body trembled as if she sat in snow, which couldn't be the case since he'd stoked the hearth fire with enough logs to heat the Parthenon.

"You are beautiful, Meg."

She crossed an arm over her chest. "I feel so… vulnerable."

His body would hate him, but he had to put Meg first. He could tame his unsated desire later with a dip in chilled water. "We don't have to do this now if you aren't ready. We can wait until we are wed."

"No. I don't want to wait." A pink tongue darted over pale lips. "I want to be joined with you, as a wife would with a husband. Tonight."

That was music to his smoldering groin. "Would you like for me to undress so we will be equally vulnerable?"

She clamped pearly teeth over her bottom lip and nodded. She would soon learn how pleasurable teething of the flesh could be. He'd promised to teach her all about making love…stage after delectable stage. This first step introduced arousal and the anticipation of more pleasing things to come.

He made quick work of buttons, buckles, and laces. His boots, socks, and shirt soon puddled at his feet. Meg's heated gasp slugged into him. He fought the urge to rush across the floor and feel the press of her naked skin against his. Slow and steady won any race.

He dragged in a calming draught of air and rose from the chair. "My trousers are next. Are you ready to have all of me bared to you?"

Her body shifted, but not her penetrating gaze. It locked onto him like a hawk on prey. "I don't know. Perhaps."

Not as ready as he'd hoped. He adopted his most reassuring expression, one that had put many a fearful orphan at ease. "There's no hurry. We can go as slow as you like."

Fingers danced over the bedsheets. "Y-your skin. It looks so smooth and sleek…like silk."

"Would you like to touch me?"

She nodded. "I would. Very much. But you will have to come to me. I-I don't think I can make my legs move right now."

"Your wish is my command." He stepped over his clothes and crossed to stand in front of her.

Blue eyes took him in, lingering on his stomach before rising to his chest. She lifted a trembling hand. Fingertips skimmed over his skin, leaving heated trails in their wake. Tremors rippled through him. He forced calm into his body, remaining still as a statute and allowing her to explore without interruption.

Her fingers traveled over him, teasing, prodding, swirling. Her exploration stopped on his upper chest. "What are these round scars?"

He briefly closed his eyes against the memory of how his young body had been tortured and maimed. His stomach roiled, and he swallowed back a bite of bile. "They are burn marks. Where my uncle stabbed me with his lit cigar."

Her face sagged. "Oh, Gabe, no. You told me your uncle was dreadful, but not this horrid. I wish I could have been there to soothe your pain."

He wished she could have been there too. Maybe a little sweetness would have tempered his building indifference to a world that had ignored his suffering. Maybe he would have made better choices as he got older.

She gathered her legs under her and rose to her knees. She leaned over and pressed gentle kisses to his scars. His heart swelled. God, he loved this woman. So full of compassion and kindness. He was the luckiest man on earth.

He cradled her chin with his hand and tilted her head back. "You are the balm to my tattered soul, Meg Myer. Let me show you just how much I love you."

Her gaze softened. "Show me. Show me all of it."

****

He stood in front of her, naked and proud. A lion, the king of his jungle. He could devour her with one bite. A shiver coursed through her. Not so much from fear as from excitement of what was to come.

"Anxious?"

His voice was soft and reassuring. She shook her head. "No. Yes. A little."

"I won't hurt you. I would never hurt you."

"I know. This is all so new to me." She averted her gaze. "I'm not sure what to do, where to look."

"Look wherever you want. There will be no censure. This is your schoolroom, a safe place to touch and taste and experience new things."

Her laugh came out sounding like a donkey braying. "I wasn't a very good student. Learning didn't come easily to me. My tutors often threw up their hands in exasperation."

"Then you had the wrong tutors." Tawny eyes twinkled. "I have an idea. Where is your hat?"

"My hat?"

"Yes, the one with the big purple feather."

"It's not in very good condition. My jaunt into the prairie left it battered and dirty."

"That doesn't matter. Where is it?"

"On the shelf in the bureau."

He wheeled around and stalked to the bureau. Lean muscles rippled with his movement. Even his buttocks were firm and tight. There was not a single ounce of sagging flesh on him. She licked lips gone dry as a summer pond. She wanted to feel his body pressed against hers, flesh to flesh, heart to heart. But she wasn't ready to jump into those waters just yet. One toe at a time would do for now.

He opened the door to the bureau and fished inside. A few seconds later, he turned with her purple hat feather clutched in his hand. His face held a most pleased expression, like a child who had been given a peppermint stick.

She focused on the bedraggled feather and not on the male appendage dangling from a nest of blond curls. "You only wanted the feather? Why?"

"Because." He closed the distance between them in three strides. "I'm going to use it for our first lesson. Now lie back on the bed."

She couldn't stop a shiver of apprehension. He was going too fast. She wanted to ease into this lovemaking process, not be mounted like a mare in the breeding pen.

"There is nothing to be frightened of, Meg. All I am going to do is brush this feather over your skin. Your body will come alive with the most pleasing sensations."

"Oh. Won't that tickle?"

"Not the way you think." He flapped the feather like a cat flicking its tail. "The experience will be more enjoyable if you are lying flat on the bed. But if that is too unsettling, you can remain sitting up."

She wagged her head. "No, I want to feel the full effect of this lesson."

She reclined back onto the bed, more curious than frightened. Gabe would never hurt her, and certainly not with a feather.

"Let's start with you facing the wall. Flip on to your side."

She rolled onto her side and stared at the papered walls. Green vines studded with pink roses meandered over a pale blue background. Though faded and peeling in some spots, the scenery instilled calm. It was as if she and Gabe were ensconced in a flower garden…their very own Eden.

The mattress dipped as a heavy weight settled beside her. Her pulse skipped. He didn't touch her, but his heat did. It wrapped around her like a blanket.

"I'm going to move your hair out of the way, all right?"

All she could manage was a nod. Every muscle in her body had coiled into a tight ball of anticipation.

His fingers pushed into her hair. Tremors shot across her scalp and skidded down her neck. She clamped down on a gasp. She didn't want him to think her a scared little peahen and put a halt to his tantalizing lesson.

He gently rolled her hair away from her neck. "Close your eyes and let go of all the negative thoughts. Concentrate on the path of the feather gliding over your skin. Are you ready?"

She nodded and closed her eyes. Something soft and light kissed her neck. The feather. It should have tickled, but it didn't. Its touch was more of an awakening of the senses. The tip trailed down her spine in a delightfully slow crusade. Her skin began to hum. Taut muscles relaxed. She sank into the mattress and opened herself up like a flower to the sunshine.

The tip continued its campaign, rolling over her ribs, sliding across her shoulder, and down her arm. Her insides quivered. She had never felt so alive.

"Feels nice, doesn't it?" At her nod, he added. "Turn onto your back. We'll awaken the rest of you."

His voice sounded ragged and breathless. She flipped onto her back and met a fiery gaze. His breaths were coming in short pants. His mouth parted. Was he going to kiss her? Her lips burned for a taste, a long thirst-quenching taste.

His chest rose as he pulled in a deep slug of air. Was he corralling his desires? She knew from watching the breeding process at Meadowdale how randy the stallions could get. The handlers struggled to keep them under control.

Tension left his face. He lifted the feather and touched the tip to her cheek. Her skin rippled. She closed her eyes, eager to be awakened to the fullest.

He traced a path to her lips. Her mouth opened of its own volition, and the feather roved over her bottom lip, slowly, enticingly. Tremors shot through her. It was a most pleasing sensation, bettered only by a kiss from his own lips.

The feather slid over her chin and coursed down her neck. The delectable stroking drifted between her breasts and slowed. Her insides began to simmer like a pot set just off the fire. She squirmed, eager to guide the feather to places that screamed for its touch.

The tip veered to the right and circled her breast, inching closer and closer to the nipple. Her skin tingled. She arched her back, wanting more, but not sure exactly what.

The feather disappeared, replaced by warm lips that took in her nipple and suckled. His tongued laved the bud. A wave of pleasure rode down her spine and pooled in her lower belly. She couldn't stopper a moan. This was the more. This was what her body clamored for.

She opened her eyes. Gabe hovered over her, his tawny locks inches from her chin. She lifted her hands and delved into his mane. Silky softness bathed her fingers. He had no imperfections. Not even in his hair.

He lifted his head, and his heated gaze locked with hers. "Are you all right? Am I going too fast?"

She drew in a ragged breath and managed to force words past a mouth squeezed dry of all moisture. "I never imagined…what you make me feel. It's…it's wonderful."

He smiled. "This is only the beginning, my love."

His love. She would never tire of hearing that. She cupped his face with both hands. "Then show me all of it, from this lovely beginning to the very end."

His smile faded. "Are you certain? Once we reach a certain point, I won't be able to stop."

"I don't want you to stop. I want your hands on my body, touching me like that feather did…bringing me to a pinnacle I can feel hovering just out of reach."

"If that's what you want, we will reach it together."

"I want."

His lips descended on hers, gentle at first, then more demanding when her mouth parted in encouragement. His tongue delved inside. She met his invasion and joined in the dance. All thoughts fled from her head. It was just the two of them encased in a cocoon of shared passion.

He cupped her breast and began tormenting her nipple with light brushes of his finger. Circling, rubbing, flicking. Heat smoldered in that secret place between her legs. The pinnacle was coming…and coming fast.

He ended their kiss and moved his mouth to her breast. His tongue continued the assault on her nipple, rubbing and flicking. The smolder between her legs leapt into a flame. She arched her hips, seeking release from the need building inside her.

His hand slid down her stomach and cupped her mound. He teased the curls with his fingers, swirling, stroking. He dipped a finger between her folds and delved inside. A bonfire erupted inside her.

"You're ready," he whispered.

More than ready. She grasped his hips and pulled him toward her. "Take me, Gabe. Take me now."

He shifted until he was hovering over her, hands on either side of her shoulders. He stilled and peered down at her. "This first time is going to hurt. But I promise, the pain will subside, and you will only feel the pleasure. Do you trust me?"

"With all my heart."

"Then let's reach that pinnacle."

Using his knee, he prodded her legs apart. Her woman's cave throbbed as if knowing what was coming. He slowly lowered himself onto her, his maleness sinking into her folds until the barrier between childhood and womanhood stopped him. They were fully united. It should have felt strange, having him inside her. But it didn't. It was as normal as breathing, and her body ached for a deep, satisfying breath.

She wiggled under him. What was he waiting for? She was ready. He was clearly ready. His hardness throbbed inside her. She opened her mouth, but before she could urge him onward, he gave a thrust of his hips. His member plunged deep. Pain blasted around his attack. She cried out and writhed her hips, seeking relief. He said there would be pain, but lordy, not this conflagration.

His mouth covered hers, his lips gently resting on hers, his breaths pulling the air from her as if to extract her pain. He slipped one hand under her buttocks, cradling her, quieting her movements.

"Hold still, my sweet. Let the ache pass."

She closed her eyes and focused on the places where their skin touched, where they were melded into one. One fire. One body. One heart. This was the closeness she had yearned for.

Ever so slowly, the fiery pain between her legs receded until all she could feel was his extraordinary fullness filling her. She gently rocked her hips. There was no answering discomfort. She rocked harder. A ribbon of pleasure unfurled inside her, twisting and coiling. She gasped and arched into the tumult.

Gabe grasped her waist and in one quick motion, rolled them over until she was sitting on top of him. Flames blazed in his eyes. His breaths were heavy and quick. He was as consumed by their joining as she was.

He slid his hands to her buttocks, fingers pressing heat into her skin. "Slow and easy, sweetheart. Or this will be over far too quickly. I want our pleasure to last."

So did she. She never wanted it to end. But something inside her cried out for release. She slid back and forth on her perch, slow and easy, like the movement in a saddle when cantering.

He matched her motion with gentle thrusts. A cauldron of need bubbled between her legs. She braced her hands on his chest and increased her pace to a full-on gallop. Her heart pounded; her head reeled. She could feel the peak glimmering just ahead, and she rode hard to reach it.

Gabe shifted beneath her. His thrusts became quicker and deeper. The ribbon inside her pulled tight. She dug her fingers into his chest, straining to find the elusive end. It came quickly and without warning. Exquisite waves unraveled inside her. A tidal wave of pleasure. She threw her head back and soared with the surge. Nothing she had ever experienced could come close to this joy. Nothing.

Gabe's hands closed over her hips. He pushed her upward and pulled himself free. A gasp whistled through clenched teeth. He bucked, and his seed spilled onto his belly. Even in the throes of passion, he was protecting her.

Chapter Twelve

Thin shafts of sunlight leeched through the gaps in the plank walls. Winter air would find entrance just as easily. The place reeked of dank earth and old wood. She paused inside the doorway and allowed her vision to adjust. A narrow, dirt aisle stretched along the length of the stable. On either side were rows of half doors leading into stalls barely large enough to stand in, much less turn around.

She pushed aside her irritation and sailed inside. Orion deserved better than this. But there was little she could do about it. Until Gabe could find a way to augment their depleted funds to pay for train passage, the shabby stable would have to suffice. It appeared the seedier side of Caldwell would be their home for a few more days.

A brown head stuck out over a stall door. It was the gelding that had valiantly toted her across the prairie despite its age and sagging back. The creature should live the rest of its short life in a pasture full of lush green grass. But that wasn't possible. Gabe had to sell the horse and his own mount in order to pay for Orion's stabling.

She pulled an apple slice from her pocket and fed it to the horse. "I'm sorry, old chap. I wish I could give you a better home than this. The stable owner seems like a nice enough man. I hope he treats you well."

The gelding flicked its tail and kept on chewing. At least it had a roof over its head and hay to eat. They all had to contend with the hand they had been dealt, for good or for bad.

She hiked her skirt out of the dirt and continued down the aisle. Nickers and soft shuffling greeted her passage. She drew in a deep, nostalgic draw of air. Stables and horses. The only things that had carried her through the long, lonely days at Meadowdale Farms. She smiled. That was before Gabe. Before their wonderous night together.

He had been amazingly tender, allaying her fears and ensuring she enjoyed every moment of their lovemaking at a pace she could accept. Warmth blossomed inside her at the memory of his skill with the feather, of his passionate kisses, and of deft fingers that found all her secret spots. He had taken her body to heights she never knew were attainable. He was tutor, conductor, and magician all rolled into one magnificent package.

Tonight would be his turn. Every lesson he had taught her would be applied to his body, including that sinfully entertaining feather. The pleasure would be all his…provided his mission to find employment was successful. Otherwise, they might be bedding in the stable with Orion.

A black head craned over the door of a stall and bounced in greeting. His forelock flapped like a duck preparing to take flight. A chuckle bubbled up from her chest. She could endure anything with Orion and Gabe by her side. A bright and happy future awaited all of them.

She fished an apple slice from her pocket and held

it out. Orion gently lipped the wedge from her palm and began chewing. Noisy, sloppy chewing. He certainly did enjoy his apples.

She went up on tiptoe and peered over the stall door. A layer of straw covered the floor. Much thinner than she would prefer, but thankfully, it appeared to be clean and dry. She drew in a breath. And fresh. After all the stallion had been through, the last thing he needed was to founder.

She rocked back onto her heels and reached up to scratch his forehead. "I'm sorry for the shoddy conditions, my precious. But I promise it won't be for long. Gabe will figure something out. He's clever and resourceful. We'll be heading for Fort Dent and a big stall thick with straw before you know it."

Orion gently butted her hand. She wagged her head and fed the horse another slice. "You don't really care where you stay, do you? As long as you can fill your belly, you are content."

The horse merely chomped on his treat. Nothing seemed to perturb the stallion. Not the kidnapping, nor the hard ride. Not even the gun battle at the soddy house had rattled the gallant horse. He remained level-headed and brave. Like Gabe.

She sighed. "He's the one, Orion. The one man I can give my heart to and not fear he will stomp on it. Sergeant Gabriel Hunt is thoughtful and trustworthy. He's my soulmate. I will love him until the day I die."

Orion blew out a cynical snort. She smiled and tickled his upper lip. "Don't worry. There's enough room in my heart for the both of you."

A barn sparrow flitted down the aisle and alit on one of the stall doors. Tufts of straw protruded from each side of its beak. Nesting material. Her home with Gabe would be just as simple. She didn't need frilly, expensive things. All she needed was him.

"We'll be married in a church filled with flowers and ribbons and tons of well-wishers. You'll be there of course. Every wedding needs a best man."

Her giddiness faltered. Would her father be one of those well-wishers? Gabe had warned her that his commander might not approve of his suit and could keep them from marrying. She squared her shoulders. He could try. But her father would fail. She and Gabe were meant to be together, and nothing and no one would come between them.

The slight shift of light at the far end of the stable caught her eye. She stilled and peered into the gloom. "Is someone there?"

Only silence answered her. She shrugged. Perhaps the movement had been from another bird or even a rodent. Even with dozens of barn cats, the stable at Meadowdale had its share of rats and mice, all searching for spilled grain.

Strong arms trapped her waist, and the familiar scent of sandalwood wrapped around her. Thoughts of rodents fled. She smiled. There was nothing to fear in these protective arms.

Warm lips pressed a kiss to her neck. "Good morning, Sunshine."

She glared at Orion. "Thanks for the warning, old boy."

The horse simply blinked and chewed on his apple slice, drool dripping from his mouth. Innocence wrapped in a shiny, black coat.

Gabe spun her around and pulled her close. "The

old boy recognizes a fellow admirer of Mistress Myer. No need to sound an alarm."

Heat thrummed through her veins. She leaned back and meet a twinkling tawny gaze. "Just an admirer?"

"Not a mere admirer. A *great* admirer."

"Is that so?"

"Let me demonstrate." He lowered his head and captured her mouth with his. Heat swirled inside her and pooled in her lower belly. Sundown couldn't get here soon enough.

A thick head butted her from behind, forcing an end to their lip-lock. She steadied herself and gave a dramatic shrug. "It appears Orion doesn't appreciate your *great* admiration, Sergeant Hunt."

"No? What about you? Do you appreciate my admiration?"

"I haven't decided yet."

The sparkle in his eyes faded. "Not having regrets, are you?"

She toyed with the buttons parading up his uniform jacket. "No regrets. Just a few lingering concerns."

"About your father."

He knew her well. "I want him to be happy for us, but I have no idea how he will react to our news."

"The general is a fair man. He will hear us out and then give it his full consideration before he answers."

"I shouldn't care how he feels…"

"But you do. He's your father. You will always care."

"I suppose."

"Well, you won't have to wonder much longer." He squeezed her waist, fingers pressing delightfully into her skin. "I was able to secure us passage on the next train out of Caldwell. We'll be in Mineral by tomorrow morning."

"How? I thought we didn't have enough money left to purchase tickets?"

"The railroad had a bounty on Sloan and his gang. Since we enabled their capture and the return of the stolen payroll, the railroad agreed to award us the reward money."

She didn't know whether to be happy or sad. Their unfettered time together was coming to an end, a very quick end. There would be no more nights of abandonment until they wed. That could be weeks, if not months.

She shook off her depressing thoughts. Sharing a life with Gabe would be worth the wait. She smiled. "That is wonderful news. Unexpected, but most welcome."

"We won't see the money for a few weeks. Until then, the Santa Fe has provided us first-class passage on the three o'clock to Guthrie. We'll have our own Pullman car, and Orion will have a private horse car filled with all the hay and oats he can eat."

She twisted her head around. "You hear that, Orion? All the oats you can eat."

The stallion bobbed his head as if in understanding. Her heart beamed. Everything was going to turn out all right. They were on their way to having that bright and happy future everyone deserved.

****

Gabe threaded his way down the aisle, swaying with the motion of the train. His step was light as his heart. He had everything he ever wanted. A lady he loved, and one who loved him in return. Their night together had been pure magic…of the ordinary kind. He had put that tantalizing purple hat feather to good use. Stroke by teasing stroke, he had brushed away Meg's nervousness until she became smoldering tinder. All it had taken was one spark and her passion had flamed into a bonfire.

Meg had been an excellent student. She learned quickly and used her newfound knowledge to turn him into a ball of heat. She had touched his body and soul like no other. He wanted more nights just like it from now until eternity.

The angel on his shoulder clucked like a disturbed rooster. Yeah, yeah. He knew. He should have told her about his gift *before* they made love. Before she was compromised. But he had been selfish. Had allowed his base desires to override his good sense. Now, if she decided his gift was not something she could live with, she had few options, and all of them unpalatable.

He hoped she could accept his unusual ability. Based on everything he knew about her; she would process his news with fairness and careful thought before passing judgment. She was her father's daughter, even if she wouldn't admit it.

Her father. *General Edward Myer.* A much trickier obstacle than his gift to navigate. The general, while a fair man, set high standards for the men under his command. He came down hard on nonconformists and idlers. Radicals in any form were not tolerated. It was one of the reasons he kept his gift a secret. He didn't want to give his commander any reason to oust him from a job that offered stability and order, things he desperately needed to keep himself on an even keel.

His gut churned. The general's requirements for a

prospective son-in-law would be even higher, if not unattainable. But he had to persevere. Not having Meg in his life would be a death sentence. Besides, after last night, even though he had pulled out before sending his seed, she could be with child. No child of his was going to grow up without a father. He would fight for them, even if it meant a discharge from the army.

He grasped the knob at the end of the railcar and pushed through the doorway and out onto the breezeway. The midmorning sun assaulted him. He squinted, momentarily blinded by the brilliant light. Before his vision could adapt, a smoke-laden gust whipped around him, tugging at his clothes and stinging his eyes and throat. He secured his hat with a hand and shortened his breaths. Life had made him tough and resilient. No smoke-belching train or uncompromising general would get the best of him. Not while he drew breath.

He aimed for the door to the adjoining railcar and managed to get his fingers on the handle. He twisted the knob and shoved inside. He paused a moment to allow his vision to adjust to the abrupt change in light. The curtains had been pulled shut, and a weak flame flickered under the lamp dome. The railcar was dim and quiet. Perhaps Meg had decided to take a nap. Her sleep the night before had been disrupted by hours of lovemaking…which he aimed to continue tonight.

He eased the door closed and moved farther inside. A sound caught his ear over the clack of iron wheels. He stilled and stared into the dimness. He could just make out a gowned figure tucked in a chair near the back of the railcar. Even in the gloom, he could sense her unease. Had she taken ill?

"What is it, Meg? What's wrong?"

"I tried to stop them…but they barged in and—"

Something poked into his back. He stiffened. There was no mistaking that hardness. It was the barrel end of a pistol.

"Hands up, Sergeant."

And no mistaking that voice. It belonged to the thug who should be behind bars in Caldwell, not skulking in dark corners on this train.

"Sloan," he ground out. "How the hell did you get free?"

The man laughed. "I have friends in many places. Come on out, Rafe."

Another man stepped from the shadows and stood behind Meg, holding a gun to her head. He had dark, fathomless eyes. Like Sloan's. Men who would kill without a second thought.

His pulse tripped. Should he comply with Sloan's demand, or go for his gun? If he ducked just right, he could avoid Sloan's bullet and get a shot off at Rafe.

He must have tensed. The gun barrel dug deeper into his spine.

"Don't try anything stupid," Sloan warned. "Or your lady friend won't see another sunrise."

Something grazed his side, and then his pistol slid from its holster, the scraping noise as emasculating as a castration. Anger rose inside him, and he drew in a calming breath. He needed a clear head if they were going to get out of this debacle unharmed.

"Hands in the air, Hunt. Slow and easy."

He slowly hefted his hands. Why had the thief put off what could be a successful escape to come after him and Meg? It didn't make any sense. If it were him, he'd be heading for Mexico on a fast horse. Perhaps that's what the man wanted.

"You can have the stallion, Sloan," he said. "Just don't hurt Miss Myer."

Her whimper cut across the short distance. He forced toughness into his expression and wagged his head. They could go after Orion later. Right now, they had to focus on staying alive.

"The black was a good ride. But it's not the horse that I want."

"What then? We don't have any money. We used all we had chasing after you."

"Not your money either. Though I heard you talking about the bounty the Santa Fe put on my head. I wouldn't count on collecting that money any time soon."

Meg gasped. "That was you. In the stable. I thought I heard someone creeping around."

"Yeah, that was me. Now that we are all enlightened as to how I knew you were on this train, walk on over to that chair beside your sweetheart." Sloan jabbed him with the pistol. "Slow and easy. I don't want to have to shoot you."

He didn't want that either. His mind whirled as he crossed to the chair. The lamp could take out Sloan, and that heavy, over-stuffed chair could subdue Rafe. He could probably manage to move both objects at the same time. But he wasn't going to risk Meg's life on *probably*. Best to bide his time and wait for a more favorable opportunity to strike.

He sank onto the chair and glared at Sloan. "Then tell me, if it's not money or the stallion, what *do* you want with us?"

"Not the both of you. Just you, Hunt."

"Me? Why me?" he asked, although he suspected he already knew the answer to that question. There had been plenty of others just like Sloan over the years…people who wanted to use him for their own gain.

Sloan's mouth twisted into a wry grin. "I saw how you called that gun to you in the thicket. I can use someone with your talent."

Ballocks, as his Irish trooper would say. Yet again, his gift, or the idea of his gift, had placed an innocent in danger. He turned his head and met a blue gaze swimming with bewilderment.

"What is he talking about, Gabe?" Lines furrowed her brow. "What did you do with a gun?"

Damn Sloan to hell. This was not how he wanted to reveal his secret. Meg needed to be eased into the notion. Not knocked over the head with it.

Sloan tut-tutted and waggled his gun. "Keeping secrets from your sweetheart isn't a wise thing to do, Sergeant."

Probably not. But no one had ever called him wise. He gave Sloan a pointed stare. If only his gift included spitting fire from his eyes, the thug would be a roasted pig.

Sloan leaned over and snagged a lace doily from a nearby end table. "Let's give the little lady a show, shall we? Call this to you."

"I don't *call* things to me."

"Then do whatever it is you do to make it come to you. Unless you're afraid of what your lady friend will think. Not many in her society are accepting of folks with abnormalities. I think they call them undesirables."

His anger returned, hard and hot. "Go to hell."

Sloan merely smiled and nodded to his henchman. Rafe thumbed back the hammer on his pistol, the clicking noise sounding like fingernails on slate. Gooseflesh crawled over his arms.

"Fine," he spat out. "I'll do it. Just don't hurt Meg."

Sloan flicked a finger at his henchman, and Rafe eased the hammer back to a less touchy position. He let go of the breath he'd been holding. Would he ever be able to live his life without being forced to do other people's bidding?

He could feel Meg's eyes boring into him. She would be shocked by what she saw. Possibly even appalled. But it couldn't be helped. He would do anything to keep her alive.

He pushed out all negative thoughts and concentrated on gathering energy in his head. Warmth swirled in his skull. His temples pulsed. He focused on the doily and held out his hand. A quick push and the lacey tuft hurled across the room and landed in his palm. He fisted it in tightly drawn fingers.

Meg's in-drawn breath sliced into him. He turned his head. Her eyes were round as dinner plates. Her bottom lip sagged. Definitely stunned.

She blinked and blinked again. "Can you move larger things? Like that lamp?"

"I can."

"Then clobber these two hooligans and get us free."

Clearly not appalled. He shook his head. "It's too dangerous. I won't put your life at risk."

"I don't care. Do it." She tilted her chin and

eyeballed the man holding a pistol to her temple. "Use whatever means you have to disable them."

The railcar pitched to the left. Sloan grunted and teetered on unsteady legs. His pistol hand wavered. Now would be the perfect time to strike. Gabe tensed and gripped the armrests.

Like a seasoned sailor, Sloan gathered his feet under him and steadied his aim. The pistol barrel shifted and pointed at Meg. "I wouldn't try anything if I were you, Hunt. You can't hit both of us at the same time."

He could. But it would be risky. Sloan appeared to be quite handy with a gun, and he'd bet the thug's henchman was just as skilled. One of them could easily get off a shot before being overpowered.

He eased back into the chair. "Don't worry, Sloan. I'm not going to try anything. You have my word."

He looked at Meg. Storm clouds had gathered on her face. Lightning shot from her eyes. She was outraged, not by what he could do, but by what he wouldn't do.

"You're just like all the other men in my life," she ground out. "Always trying to protect me. Always doing what you think is right for me. You're nothing but a coward."

Chapter Thirteen

She paced from the door to the window and back. Gabe was one special man. He had a talent like no other she had ever seen. Unfortunately, he was damned foolish about it. He could have used his gift to free them from Sloan's clutches. But no. He had to protect her. Now, Sloan had him performing like a bear in a circus, doing things that could get him arrested or even killed.

When the train stopped in Guthrie, Sloan had made them disembark, and to her relief, had unloaded Orion as well. The polecat had threatened to kill all three of them if she or Gabe caused any trouble. As much as she wanted to run to the nearest law authority, she had no choice but to cooperate. She could not lose the two most valuable things in her life.

She closed her eyes and leaned back against the door frame. Why did everything good in her life have to go sour? Was that bright and happy future she envisioned just an illusion? Every time she thought the sun would finally shine, storm clouds appeared. She must be cursed. That was it. Instead of blessings, her birth had been anointed with misfortune so that any living thing she touched withered and died. Her mother, Sam, and now Gabe. All taken from her.

A sob caught in her throat. She sank to the floor and hugged her knees. Tears burned in her eyes. She couldn't lose Gabe. She just couldn't. Surely God wouldn't give her happiness only to yank it away. She had never intentionally harmed a soul. Her heart was good and pure and full of giving. She didn't deserve such a blight. Neither did Orion or Gabe. Suffering should be reserved for those whose souls were full of evil and hatred, like Sloan. Those sorts would always be searching for fulfillment and never find it, no matter how hard they tried.

The lamp flickered, the flame dying down to a nub and then blazing back. There was no breeze, so the oil must have impurities, tiny bits that arrested the fire until the good oil could prevail.

She scrubbed tears from her eyes. Maybe she was looking at this tragedy in the wrong light. Maybe her torments were lessons, steps on a staircase that she must climb to reach the happiness she sought. The incident with Sam had brought her father back into her life. The kidnapping of Orion had led to an unexpected closeness with her escort. Therefore, this enforced captivity could be just another rung she must scale.

Her despair evaporated, and she pushed upright. In order to climb the ladder to enlightenment, she first had to find a way out of the hotel room without alerting the guard. Sloan had stationed his henchman in the hallway outside her door to ensure Gabe's full cooperation. If Rafe didn't receive word from his leader at prearranged intervals, he was to kill her. She glared at the door. That was not going to happen. Not while she could put one foot in front of the other.

She pressed an ear to the wood. There was only silence coming from the other side. But that didn't mean Sloan's henchman wasn't out there. Sloan had called him Rafe, and the man appeared to be unswervingly loyal. She had tried every trick she could think of to convince him to let her go. Christina would have applauded her flirtatious wheedling; little good it had done. The thug had only grunted at her attempts.

She tapped a finger to her lips. The motion seemed to help Sam come up with solutions to thorny problems. She could only hope it would do the same for her.

So how to escape without causing harm to herself, Gabe, or Orion? If only she had Gabe's power. She wouldn't hesitate to use it. Moving objects with one's mind was truly extraordinary. Why had he concealed such a gift from her? Did he believe her too small-minded to handle such a revelation? Worse, did he not trust her to keep his secret?

She had called him a coward. That had been a little harsh. He was the bravest man she knew. But rage and a huge dose of fear had filled her head. She couldn't stop the ugly words from tumbling free. She was still angry at him. She stalked to the dresser and doused the lamp. They could discuss his rationale for concealing his gift from her later, after they were all safe, and Sloan and his thug were behind bars. Right now, she had an escape to plan.

She moved to the window and pulled back the curtain. Night had fallen over the town. The street was dark and void of any traffic. Only scattered slashes of lamplight lit the windows of the buildings lining the roadway. If Sloan had posted additional guards outside the hotel, then darkness would be her best hope at fleeing undetected.

Just below her window, a portico roof jutted out over the hotel entrance. It was steep and probably slippery if the shine on the tin was any indication. But it appeared to be the only way down. She would just have to go slow and use extra caution. Not an easy task when all she wanted to do was leap out the window and be gone.

She slipped her fingers under the window and slowly lifted. Wood screeched on wood. *Rooster feathers*. She stopped and listened. No sounds came from the door. Rafe must not have heard the noise. Good. She inched the window further open, stopping when the screeching grew too loud.

Once the opening was large enough for her to fit through, she halted her efforts. The tinkle of piano music rode the night air. Two figures crossed into the lamplight on the street below. A scantily dressed woman hung onto the arm of her escort, a man in a top hat who could barely put one foot in front of the other. The man faltered and sank to one knee. The woman's throaty laugh rang out as she attempted to help the man rise. Meg nodded. Hopefully that little vaudeville show would distract any guards that might be lurking below.

She drew the back of her skirt between her legs and tucked it into her waistband, fashioning a sort of pantaloons. She then kicked off her slippers and removed her stockings. The chill would be uncomfortable, but bare feet would make navigating the slippery roof much easier. And quieter. She'd learned these tricks back at Meadowdale when she'd slipped from her room at night to go fishing with Sam.

Sam. Guilt slammed into her. Thoughts of him had been few and far between over the past few weeks. Finding Orion and her blossoming relationship with Gabe had consumed her. She could only hope her friend found someone as special to love. Well, maybe not as *gifted* special. Just special.

She listened one last time for any sounds coming from the doorway, and hearing none, she slipped a leg through the window opening. Her toes met cold metal. She froze and bit down on a gasp. It was much icier than expected. But there was nothing for it. A little discomfort would be worth saving the ones she loved.

She ducked under the half-open window and crawled out onto the roof. The laughing woman and her escort had regained their equilibrium and were moving on. The show was over. There was no time to waste.

Meg inched over to the far side of the roof and slid down the slope on her rear, gripping the slick tin with her heels and flattened hands. After what seemed an eternity, her toes met open air. She rolled onto her stomach and eased over the edge. Legs dangling, she glanced at the street below. Nothing but hard dirt to break her fall. Not ideal. But better than something large like a rock or a water trough.

She wriggled until her hips slipped over and then her stomach. She gave a final push and dropped the rest of the way down. Her feet slammed into the ground with a jolt. She crouched and rolled with the motion. Another ploy she'd learned at Meadowdale to lessen the impact of a fall.

Heart thudding, she pushed upright and scurried out of the street and onto the boardwalk. She plastered her back against the porch post and waited. No shouts or hurried footfalls rushed to overtake her. The only movement came from a shadow cast into the street from inside the hotel. She heaved a sigh of relief. A miracle in a month fraught with ill luck.

She untucked her skirt and shook out the dirt and creases. It would take a week of soaking to get the grime out of her clothes and off her skin. Fortunately, the task ahead didn't require pretty. Just speed and stealth.

To the right of the hotel was nothing but trade shops, saloons, and the stable where they'd dropped off Orion. She had noted the buildings during their trek from the train station. There had been no sign of a sheriff's office. She pushed away from the post and headed to the left. Surely, she would find one this way. A town this size would need someone to maintain law and order.

Her footfalls thumped softly on the boardwalk. The planks were a bit rough and uneven in spots, but still navigable if one took care. She hurried through the patches of lamplight and used caution when crossing through the dark stretches. A stubbed toe would stop her in her tracks.

The sounds of debauchery dimmed. Saloons and hotels gave way to mercantiles and residential homes. A large display window held an assortment of bonnets and hats. Any other time she would linger and gawk. Not now. Not with so many lives at stake.

She glanced over her shoulder. The boardwalk remained still and quiet. Her escape appeared to have gone undetected. She squashed her excitement. She wasn't out of the woods yet. She still had to find the sheriff.

As she stepped off the boardwalk to cross to the next block, a two-story building on the other side of the street caught her eye. A large placard perched over the doorway. *Sheriff.* She heaved a sigh of relief. She'd made it, and the lawman appeared to be in, if glowing windows and the horses tied to the hitching rail out front were any indication.

She gathered a handful of skirt and plowed across the street. Ruts and dirt clumps did their best to stop her, but she managed to reach the other side without wrenching an ankle. Once on the boardwalk, she rushed toward the brightly lit building. A bay with black stockings snorted at her as she passed the hitching rail. She took a closer look. All the horses were equipped with McClellan saddles and blue blankets edged in gold. United States Army issue. She'd seen the same tack on cavalry mounts that had performed at an exhibition at Fort Lyon years ago. Wonderful. It appeared the sheriff had a ready-made posse.

She grasped the doorknob and pushed inside. The hum of conversation abruptly halted, and a dozen pair of eyes turned in her direction. Most of the men wore army blue uniforms just like Gabe's. Hands rose and swept off hats. A group standing in the middle of the room stepped aside, giving her a clear view of a large wooden desk. Behind it stood two men, one wearing civilian clothes, the other a uniform with gold embroidered shoulder bars holding two stars. The officer's eyes caught and held her gaze. They were pale blue and framed by short-cropped gray hair. His nose turned up slightly at the end as hers did. There was no mistaking his likeness. He embodied the portrait hanging in the hallway at Meadowdale. Her pulse hopscotched.

General Edward Myer. Her father.

****

Night had fallen over the town. Not that he could

see the darkness. He could hear it. The clink of piano music, the throaty laughter, and the drone of men at their cards and drink. A quiet evening. But that could change at the drop of a hat.

Two years ago, just like now, it had been early in the evening at the Blue Dog Saloon in Dodge City. The piano player sat on his stool, rocking to the music that poured from beneath long, string bean-like fingers. He wore a red and white striped shirt with red suspenders. He remembered that shirt because once the shooting ended, there was no white to be seen, only red.

A disagreement had arisen at a table next to his. The foursome had been at their cards and whiskey since well before he arrived. Two of them were dust-covered from the trail. Drovers, he had suspected. The other two were clean-shaven and well-dressed. An angry voice had risen over the din. Something about aces and cheating. Chair legs scraped against the wood floor as the two drovers leapt to their feet, guns drawn. In a matter of seconds, bullets were flying.

He and his fellow players had leapt for cover under their table. The scrabble of running feet and shattering glass had boiled around them as if someone had upended a bucket of bloody slops in the middle of a pack of wild boars. Chaos and confusion filled the room.

He could sure use a ruckus about now. Anything to distract Sloan so he could get a jump on him.

The toe of his boot struck something hard. He stumbled and struggled to stay upright, a difficult task with his hands bound behind his back. The blindfold didn't help. It made righting himself all the harder. He collided into what felt like a post. Pain shot through his shoulder, and a groan slid past his lips.

A beefy hand shackled his arm. "Stop bumbling about and making all that racket."

Anger overrode the fear choking his throat. He couldn't stop his irritation from blasting out. "If you take off this damn blindfold, I'll be able to walk better. Make less noise."

"Not going to happen. I know what you can do when you lay your eyes on something." Sloan gave him a shove. "Get moving."

He lurched forward but managed to keep his feet under him. His stride evened out, as did his control. A head filled with rage would only hinder his quest to get free.

"Why the hurry, Sloan? You got someplace we need to be?"

"Off the street. Now shut your yapper and keep moving. You talk more than an old maid at a social."

Sloan had a sense of humor. Sarcastic, but still comical. It might be an edge he could use later.

A sliver of light gleamed from beneath the bottom edge of the blindfold. His stumble into the post must have knocked the cloth askew. Good. He would take any advantage luck saw fit to throw his way.

He tilted his head back and strained to see what lay ahead. Every muscle in his body itched to fight. But he held himself in check. Rashness often led to mistakes. He would rein in his impatience and wait for the perfect opportunity. For now, he would shuffle along, pretending to be blind and helpless.

The undulating boardwalk evened out. Bawdy night sounds faded. They were headed away from the seedier section of town. Away from the hotel where

Sloan had stashed Meg. His gut churned. How was she faring? Had they bound her? Gagged her? Red sizzled in his vision. If one hair on her head was harmed, Sloan and his thug would pay for it...dearly.

Not that his retaliation would make a difference. She had already called him a coward. Maybe he was. But if holding back kept her safe, then he would accept her contempt.

"Goddammit to hell," Sloan muttered.

The talon gripping his arm tugged him sideways and thrust him against a wall. His nose mashed into unforgiving wood. He turned his head to the side and struggled to draw a breath. Cold steel pressed into his skull.

"Be still, or I'll take you out right here."

He calmed and listened. The faint clop of hooves dusted the air. Horses. A dozen or more and moving at a quick clip. One of the riders said something, but it was too muffled to make out.

After a few minutes, the thumping faded and then vanished. The pressure on his back and skull eased. He pulled in deep breaths, feeding his air-starved lungs.

"All right, Hunt. Move on. Slowly now. No fast moves."

Not a problem. His movements would be anything but fast. The blindfold had slipped back in place, shutting off his limited view and killing any advantage he might have had. Damn. Damn. Damn. If it wasn't for bad luck, he'd have none.

Three dozen steps and two lurches later, Sloan pulled him to a stop. The faint screech of hinges sounded, and then he was shoved to the right. The blackness behind the blindfold lightened. Warm air closed around him, heating his chilled skin. Their footfalls changed from soft thumps to dull echoes. They had entered a building of some sort.

The door clicked shut. "Douse the light, Tucker," Sloan muttered.

"What's going on?" came another voice.

"Soldiers. About ten of them just rode by with the sheriff."

So that's what had put Sloan on edge. Wonder what regiment they were from and why they were in Guthrie? Fort Dent was about seventy miles to the southwest. Fort Smith about a hundred and seventy-five to the east. That small a patrol could be out for any number of reasons.

A soft spluttering sounded, and then darkness returned. Sloan herded him across the floor. The heat bathing his skin intensified. He was nearing the source, possibly a potbelly stove or some other enclosed apparatus since there was little to no light detectable through the blindfold.

Four, five, six steps. Sloan pulled him to a stop. "That's far enough. There's a chair behind you. Sit down and keep quiet."

He backed up until his calves met something solid. He slowly squatted and met the hard, flat seat of a chair. He settled in and leaned back. His arms and shoulders screamed in protest. Even his wrists wanted in on the hollering. He ignored the pain and focused on gathering any information that might help him escape.

The smell of burning wood and ash filled the room. He drew in a deep breath. Musty and stale. Wherever Sloan had him stashed, the place hadn't been used in a while.

Boot heels thumped away. There wasn't much of an echo. Must be a small room with a low ceiling. Knowing his luck, there was only one way out, and it would be well guarded.

"See anything?" Sloan asked.

The place had at least one window. There had been no squawk of hinges indicating his captors watched through a cracked opening in the doorway. The window could be the way out. Glass was a flimsy barrier. Crashing through would be noisy and potentially bloody, but it could be done.

"All's quiet right now," Tucker answered.

Not old. Not young. Middle-aged. Probably just as hardened as his *jefe*. He wouldn't find mercy with either man.

Chair legs scraped across the floor and drew next to him. The noise stopped and then wood squealed in protest of a heavy weight. Someone had set up camp next to him. Damn. He wouldn't be able to work his hands free of the rope without being observed.

"You take the first watch," Sloan said. "I'm going to put my feet up and have a quick siesta. Wake me if you see that patrol returning."

"Sure thing. What are you gonna with that one? Hold him for ransom or something?"

Gabe grunted. If only that was all Sloan wanted him for. He'd pay the bounty himself if that was the case.

"He's joining our gang. Got some skills we can put to good use."

"He good with a gun?"

"Something better than that."

196

Chapter Fourteen

"What were you thinking, Meggie?"

While said without malice, the censure still pinched. Not even the use of her pet name could ease the hurt. She swayed on weedy legs. The chair in front of her offered mooring. She gripped the back and dug her fingers into the top slat.

"My horse had been stolen from me." She forced hardness into a voice that sought to quiver. "I wanted him back."

"But to race off into the wilderness. By yourself. With no chaperone and no protector. It was reckless and dangerous."

"No one else would go after Orion. I had to do it myself."

"You put your life in jeopardy for a horse?"

Not a single gray hair moved with the wag of his head. Everything about her father shouted composure. From his stone-faced greeting to his pedestrian words. She wanted to shout and pound that lifeless blue chest with her fists. She gouged the chair wood instead.

"He is not just a horse. He's everything to me. Orion was there for me at Meadowdale when I most needed support."

"If the horse meant that much to you, I would have sent a patrol after him. All you had to do was ask."

He would send a patrol after Orion, not go himself,

just as he had done with her. Frustration and hurt festered inside her. Even though it was just the two of them in the sheriff's office, the room felt stuffy and congested. Breathing came only with effort. She drew in a deep, fortifying bolt of air.

"How could I have known what you would do? You never concerned yourself with my welfare before the incident with Sam. You never sent for me until you were forced to do so. And then, instead of collecting me yourself, you sent your minion." The persistent quiver finally stole up her throat. "Th-that…told me *exactly* what I meant to you."

"You mean the world to me."

Was that a crack in his voice? Couldn't be. His eyes were cool as a cloudless winter sky. And his lips remained pulled into the same thin line that had welcomed her arrival in the office. She was a disappointment. Fine. That shoe fit on any foot.

She shoved up her chin. "You have an odd way of showing it, General Myer."

Furrows dug into his brow and tucked around his eyes. His shoulders went back, squaring off against her attack. "I wanted to collect you, but a situation arose with a local Indian tribe that required my attention. I couldn't leave the garrison. I trusted Sergeant Hunt to see you home safely. In hindsight, I suppose that faith was misplaced. He should not have allowed you to engage in such foolish behavior."

"Believe me, Gabe tried everything short of hog-tying me to a chair. But I refused to give in. He finally realized the wisest course of action was to go along and keep me safe."

"Gabe. That's the third time this evening you have

called Sergeant Hunt by his given name." Knowing eyes drilled into her. "Have you come to care for him?"

Her insides twisted. She wanted Gabe by her side when they told her father about their relationship…a united front to combat his reaction. Until that time, she would carefully couch her answers.

She detached from the wood slat and rounded the chair. She settled on the seat, fluffing out her skirts and using the interval to prepare her thoughts. She didn't want to inadvertently say the wrong thing and prejudice his judgment against them.

The lamp on the desktop flickered. Macabre shadows danced on the walls. Eerie, death-like shadows. An omen? A shudder rippled through her. She prayed not.

She sucked in another bolstering breath and looked up and into a surprisingly gentle gaze. His mouth had softened. Even the firm set to his head held a curious tilt.

"You look just like her," he said, his tone soft almost tender.

"Look like whom?"

"Your mother. Same mouth. Same fine cheekbones. You even pull your composure around you like a cloak. She did that. Often. I admired that in her."

"Yes, well…" She cleared her throat of the cotton that had suddenly sprouted. She wasn't ready to talk about her mother. Not yet. Not with him.

"Your faith in Sergeant Hunt was not misplaced," she said. "He has been a Godsend throughout this entire ordeal. I came to rely on his wisdom and unwavering support. Orion and I wouldn't be here without him."

"I am pleased to hear it. My assessment of the men

under my command is rarely wrong."

That cloak of composure he admired slipped. Desperation shivered on her tongue. "Y-you will find him, won't you, Father?"

"We will do everything within our power to locate him. However…" His expression turned preacher solemn. "You should be prepared for a long wait. Sheriff Hobson says Sloan's bunch has eluded every attempt at capture. It could take weeks, possibly even months to track him down."

Weeks. Months. Her insides churned. What if they never found him? What if she never heard Gabe's deep, intoxicating voice again? Never felt his loving touch? They might as well put her in a pine box.

She straightened the stack of papers on the desktop and aligned the pen next to the ink well. *A tidy house makes for a tidy mind,* Aunt Alma always said. She needed her mind clear of clutter, else she would suffocate.

A noise drifted in from the street. She jerked up her head and stared at the darkened window. Was her father's patrol returning? After hearing about her and Gabe's plight, he had sent his soldiers with the sheriff to the hotel where she had been held captive. Hopefully, they would apprehend Rafe without bloodshed and persuade him to provide information on where Sloan had taken Gabe.

Her father crossed to the window and cupped hands on the panes. He turned his head from side to side, peering out into the darkness. Anticipation frolicked in her veins.

"Do you see anything?" she blurted. "Is it your patrol?"

"There's no sign of them. But it's still early yet. Apprehending an armed criminal cannot be rushed, else everyone involved could be placed in danger."

"Of course." Gabe wouldn't want anyone to be hurt at his expense. She would just have to be patient...not her best attribute.

A deafening silence fell over the room. Her father stayed at the window, still as a statue and staring out into the darkness. He had tucked his hands behind his back, shoulders squared, a perfect barricade. A million questions raced in her head. Why was he so distant, so cold? What had she ever done to earn his indifference? A hard knot of yearning gathered in her throat.

"I never intended to hurt you, Meggie."

Guilt and sadness smeared his voice. He continued staring out the window as if looking at her was too difficult. She wanted to offer comfort but wasn't sure how or where to begin.

"Father—"

"No. Let me finish." He wheeled around and scrubbed a hand through his hair, mussing the neatly combed strands. "After your mother passed, I was lost. I didn't know how to give you the things you needed. The things you deserved. I had no idea how to raise a child."

She anchored trembling fingers on the edge of the desk. "What I needed, Father...what I desired most in all the world, was your love."

He heaved a sigh. One of those long, drawn-out breaths where the soul rides out on a charging black steed. "My sister never told you about us, about our past, did she?"

"Aunt Alma was as distant and uncaring as you

are."

His shoulders slumped as if bearing a great weight. "Don't blame Alma for her lack of emotion. She never learned how to care for others. Our mother, your grandmother, died giving us life. Our father blamed us for taking his beloved wife from him. We were abandoned, physically and emotionally. Our only source of contact came from a nanny whose idea of affection was a stout stick."

He had been abused. Horribly. Just like Gabe. She should resent her father's treatment of her. Should continue to hold him to account. But her journey with Gabe had taught her that anger and bitterness were shackles that only held her back. The love she sought could be hers if she trusted in herself and opened her heart.

She cast off the chains of her past. Her father needed her. Needed her love and comfort. And more importantly, she needed him. She rose to her feet but paused when he held up a hand.

"There's more. Not that it absolves my behavior, but hopefully it helps you understand." He fingered a gold jacket button. "I left that house of darkness as soon as I was old enough and joined the army. For the first time in my life, I found acceptance. The discipline and order of the military became my lifeline. I devoted everything I had in me to becoming the best officer and commander. There was nothing left in my heart for anything or anyone else."

"What about Mother? You must have loved her."

"I provided for her. Gave her the things she needed. She accepted what I had to offer and didn't ask for more. I respected her for that."

Understand what he was saying? Yes. Accepting of it. Absolutely not. She crossed the floor in three quick strides and rested a hand on his arm. "Well, I am asking for more. I want to forge a new relationship with you, Father. One where we both learn to love and trust one another. I believe, given time and patience, we can have that."

Blue eyes glistened with watery emotion. Tears. A promising sign. His heart *could* be touched through all that armor.

The thud of horse hooves burst in from outside, followed by the muffled sound of voices. He claimed her hand and gently tugged her toward the door.

"It's the patrol. Let's see what they found."

The racing of her heart matched the quick shuffle of her bare feet. She paused only a moment while he twisted the knob and threw open the door. He stepped out onto the boardwalk, and she tucked in beside him.

The soldiers had dismounted and were herding a dark-haired man toward the building. *Rafe*. Lamplight greased his face. One eye was swollen shut and dried blood caked the side of his mouth. He walked with a noted limp. He must have needed extra *coercion* to provide the information the soldiers required. She grunted under her breath. Nothing less than what the skunk deserved.

"Well," her father asked. "What did you find out, Sergeant?"

One of the soldiers stepped forward and snapped a brisk salute. "It took a while, General, sir, but he finally gave us something useful. Said Sloan is holding Sergeant Hunt in a farmhouse about fifteen miles outside of town. We were just about to head that way."

"Excellent. Bring me my horse. I will ride with you."

Excitement sang in her veins. Gabe would soon be back by her side. She started to step off the boardwalk, but a hand on her arm stopped her.

"Where are you going, Meggie?"

She looked up and into a concerned blue gaze. Odd how familiar those eyes were. It was as if she were peering into a mirror. "I'm going to collect Orion so I can come with you."

"It's too dangerous. You should wait here with the sheriff until we return."

"But I want to be there when you free Gabe."

"I know you do, but it's not a sensible thing to do. Sloan won't give up without a fight. You could be hurt or worse." He gave her arm a gentle squeeze. "I want a chance to make things right with you, to forge that new relationship you spoke of. I can't do that if anything happens to you. Please heed my advice and stay here."

Those very same words uttered by Gabe weeks ago had fallen on deaf ears. But she had learned to love and trust him. If she ever hoped to have the same with her father, she would have to listen.

"Very well. I will do as you suggest and wait here with the sheriff." A lump caught in her throat. She grasped his arm and squeezed. "Please bring Gabe back safe and sound, Father. Please."

"I will, Meggie darling. On my honor, I will."

The sheriff approached, herding a rope bound Rafe in front of him. The thug's dark gaze sliced into her. A gleam lit his good eye as if he held onto a decadent secret. One corner of his mouth lifted into a smirk. Her stomach roiled. Something was wrong. Something that might get someone she loved killed.

****

Braided hemp dug into his wrists. His skin jangled with the pricks of a hundred needles. Raw. Probably bleeding, too. He wriggled harder. Pain didn't matter. What mattered was getting free. Getting to Meg before Sloan or his henchmen did. He wasn't going to lose a future he'd only just realized he could have...provided she still wanted him.

Meg didn't seem to be disturbed by the revelation of his gift. In fact, she had urged him to use it. Had even become angered when he didn't. Funny how he'd tried so hard all his life to be normal and accepted, and now because of his refusal to use his gift, he'd been rejected.

"Do you want to go back to your siesta, boss? I can keep an eye on the soldiers and wake you if there's any movement."

Gabe groaned under his breath. The snoring emanating from the napping beast had nearly split his eardrums. He could barely think over the din. But it had provided the perfect cover for his efforts with the rope bindings.

Sloan's grunt humped across the short distance. "That damn chair is harder than a weathered whore. No, I'm awake now. Might as well stay that way. If the soldiers start moving again, we want to be ready to act."

Tucker had roused Sloan from his nap when the soldiers returned with the sheriff. The two men had cursed the sight of their comrade being herded into the jailhouse, bound and gagged. Rafe had been apprehended. Good. One thug down. Two to go.

The only silver lining to the whole debacle was that

Meg was safely tucked inside the jailhouse. Sloan's irritation had intensified when he spotted her greeting the arriving soldiers. She had somehow escaped from the hotel and made her way to the sheriff's office. He couldn't be prouder of her. She had more gumption in her little finger than many soldiers he knew. The only problem…her courage had put her in Sloan's crosshairs.

The bastard had spit and fumed. Said he would get Rafe free and, in the process, nab Meg. Said she would pay for flouting his instructions. His gut clenched at the thought of what Sloan might do to her. He had to get free before that happened.

A soft scrape sounded and then bootheels thumped across the floor toward him. He halted his efforts. He couldn't risk being caught. The bindings were still as tight as they had been when Sloan first tied them.

"You know, I thought you had gone loco, boss," Tucker said from the other side of the room.

A metal squeal rang out, and then a gold sliver of light gleamed through the cotton blindfold. It was Sloan opening the door to the potbelly stove. Probably to stoke the fire. The room had gone chilly, for more reasons than one.

"Is that so?" Sloan muttered.

"Yup. I wondered what the hell you were thinking when you told me to find a place across from the sheriff's office to hole up in. Now I see why. We can watch all their comings and goings."

"Exactly." A faint thump sounded, then came the crackle of spitting embers and energized flames. "We can make our plans based on what they do. When they go looking for us, and I have no doubt they will, they won't expect us to be hiding right under their noses."

Gabe gave a grunt of his own. The only plan these two needed to make was how to pack for a long, hot stint in hell.

"Wait...there's movement. The soldiers are starting to mount up." Tucker's voice hitched. "You think Rafe told them where we're at?"

The door to the potbelly stove clanged shut. "Rafe knows better than that. He'll send them on a wild goose chase. What about the girl. Is she with them?"

"I don't see her. Looks like she went back inside with the sheriff."

"Good. We'll kill two birds with one stone."

Kill. He didn't like the sound of that. Footsteps retreated to the other side of the room and then quieted. Silence swallowed the room. All he could hear was the rush of his racing blood.

"Good, they're gone," Sloan said. "Head over to the Gold Nugget, Tucker. You should find Buck and Clem Craven there. Tell them Sloan needs them for a job. I'll make it worth their while."

"Sure thing, boss."

The faint screech of hinges sounded. Night sounds drifted in and then faded with the thud of the shutting door. That left him and Sloan. Odds he could handle.

"You're wasting your time, Hunt."

He mimicked Sloan's grunting disregard. "Is that so?"

"You ain't gonna get free of them ropes," Sloan said. "My daddy taught me how knots could be tied good and tight. No amount of struggling will loosen them."

An underlying hardness coated Sloan's voice. He

poked at it. "I'll bet you know first-hand about being tied up. Your daddy do that?"

Only cricket chirps greeted his prodding. Struck a chord it appeared. Maybe he could use their mutual mistreatment to his advantage.

"I feel your pain, Sloan. After my parents died, my sister and I were sent to live with my mother's brother. Old bastard never had any children of his own. His idea of raising kids was to give daily beatings and lock us in a closet for days without food or water."

A soft scrape sounded and then came the crackle of a flame. Sloan took in several sucking draughts. A few seconds later, the smell of tobacco smoke stung his nostrils. Memories surfaced of being stabbed over and over with a lit cigar. His gut clenched. Seemed like he was always at the mercy of some mad man.

Sloan pushed out a long puff. "How'd your ma and pa die?"

The knot in his stomach tightened. Talking about his parents always dredged up ugly feelings of hurt and helplessness. He never wanted to feel that way again. But if sharing his past got Sloan to warm up to him, then he would deal with the nastiness.

"My father was killed hunting a wild boar. The thing turned on him. Sliced him with its tusks. He bled out sitting under an old oak tree. A year later, my mother passed away. The doctor said a lung illness did her in. I say she died of a broken heart."

A lump formed in his throat. To have that kind of deep, abiding love was the one thing he had always dreamed of having. He knew in his heart he'd found it with Meg. He just needed to get out of the cage he and everyone else tried to put him in.

Sloan took another draw on his cigar. "Mine got swept away in a mudslide. Rain came down for weeks on end. Turned the ground into a muddy mire. The hillside behind our house gave way. I managed to get on the roof and ride to safety. My parents were never found."

"That's unfortunate. Did your kinfolk take you in?"

"Didn't have any. The law tried to put me in an orphanage, but I wasn't having any of it. Mean ol' bitches ran that place. I took off and never looked back."

Just like him, Sloan had been forced to take care of himself at a young age. He'd learned to do whatever it took to survive and do it quickly. It was a dark and lonely path, one that led to self-destruction. If it weren't for the wise and loving caretakers at Seaton House, he could be the one with the empty soul.

He leaned into the ropes strapping his chest. "That cigar smells mighty fine. Got another one? I could use a good smoke after dredging up all those old memories."

Sloan's snort axed the air. "I might be ugly, but I ain't stupid."

That remained to be seen. He kept his voice even and amiable. "You don't have to take off the blindfold. Just untie my hands so I can enjoy a smoke."

"Ain't gonna happen."

"What's the harm? You have all the advantages. Unrestrained and armed. Not much I can do against that."

"And it's going to stay that way. You'll just have to enjoy your smoke second-hand."

Footfalls drew closer, stopped, and then thumped away, trailed by the scrape of what sounded like chair legs on the floor. Once the noise reached the other side of the room, it ended. Chair wood squealed and then quiet fell over the room. Sloan must have set up camp by the window so he could keep watch. It's what he would do if he were being hunted.

Minutes ticked by. Only the sound of Sloan puffing on his cigar broke the quiet. Gabe resumed his wrestle with the rope. He wasn't going to give up. His path shimmered with a bright and loving light, and he wasn't about to veer away from it.

"Well, well. What do we have here?" Sloan's manic guffaw slugged the air. "It appears our little birdy has flown the coop."

Footfalls rapped the floor, then came the squeal of the opening door. Silence fell over the room. Sloan had left. It was now or never.

He twisted and wrenched, using hands, arms, and body…anything to gain an advantage over the unrelenting tautness. Nothing worked. The rope held tighter than a pair of steel shackles. Damn Sloan's vile daddy.

The shuffle of footsteps bounced into the room. Two people. Maybe three based on the hurried taps and thumps. Door hinges squawked and then the door slammed shut. His reprieve was over, and he hadn't made a dent in the bindings. Could his luck get any worse?

A soft grunt sliced the air, and then came a familiar voice. "Let me go, you oaf."

His heart and escape efforts stopped cold. It appeared his luck had indeed worsened.

****

Her heart thudded against her ribs, sending chilled

blood coursing through her veins. Her knees wobbled. She shoved hardness into a body that wanted to curl into a ball. She would not cower.

She twisted her arm, trying to elude the hand fettering her arm. "Let go of me, I said. I'm not one of your painted whores to be man-handled about."

Her captor ignored her struggles and dragged her farther into the room. She scrambled to stay upright. The last thing she wanted was to be on her back and at his mercy.

Only a shard of light spilling through the window lit the room. It was small and smelled of musk and cigar smoke. There were no locks or steel bars, but because of her ineptitude, it was now her jail.

She knew Rafe had lied about Sloan's whereabouts, but she never expected the criminal to be hiding within spitting distance of the sheriff's office. If she had, she would have been more vigilant. Panic clawed at her throat. What was Sloan going to do now that she was back under his control? He'd warned that if she tried to escape, he would kill Gabe. She swallowed back the bitter taste of bile. She wouldn't let that happen. Couldn't. Gabe was her world, and she wasn't going to let anyone take that away.

She dug in her heels and managed to regain her balance and her composure. "What have you done with Sergeant Hunt?" she spat out. "If you have hurt him, I'll make sure you pay for it. Most horribly."

Sloan shoved her onto a chair resting under the window. "You'll find out soon enough. Sit there and don't move. And for God's sake, shut your trap. All that yammering hurts my ears."

She gripped the chair seat, anchoring her anger. He

had the upper hand with his brute strength and that pistol he had poked into her spine. But she would get free eventually. She would bet her life on it. And once she was done with him, aching ears would be the least of his pains.

"Meg, I'm over here."

Her heart leapt at the familiar voice. She wrenched her head around and squinted into the darkness. She could just make out the silhouette of a man sitting in a chair on the other side of the room.

"Gabe. Are you all right?"

"I'm fine. What about you? Did Sloan or his thug hurt you?"

"Just my pride is injured. I managed to escape from Rafe…" She glared up at Sloan. "But I fell right into this one's hands."

"You sure did, pretty lady. Easiest bird I've snared in years."

He met her scowl with a smug sneer. She bristled. If only she had a pistol, she'd shoot the thug between his beady, black eyes.

"Why did you leave the safety of the sheriff's office?" Gabe asked. "Did something happen to force you out? Did Rafe get free?"

"No. But he was being very difficult. Yelling and banging about. I didn't want to distract the sheriff while he dealt with the maniac. Moreover, I didn't want anyone trying to stop me."

"Stop you from doing what?"

"From collecting Orion so I could catch up to Father and warn him about Rafe's deceit."

"That's enough yapping," Sloan barked. "The two of you can talk turkey later."

"The general is here in Guthrie?" Gabe asked.

She glanced at Sloan. He didn't appear to be riled by Gabe's flouting of his edict. "Yes, he and his men are on their way to a house outside of town where Rafe said Sloan was holding you. Just as I suspected, the thug lied."

Sloan's ugly laugh stained the air. "You didn't really think my man would give me up that easily, did you?"

"It doesn't matter." She treated him to a pointed look. "Once my father discovers you are not at that farmhouse, he'll come back and search this entire town. General Edward Myer won't stop until he finds you."

"General Myer can search all he wants. I'll be long gone by then. We all will."

Did that mean leaving dead or alive for her and Gabe? Fear poked holes in her courage. "What are you going to do with us?"

"Don't know yet. I need to think on it. Besides, the two of you seem to have mud in your ears."

"What does that mean?"

"It means you don't listen very well. Now shut up before I shut you up." Sloan glared across the room. "That means the both of you."

No sound came from the far side. Satisfied with Gabe's compliance Sloan turned to the window. He peered through the panes, like a vulture searching for something rotten to gorge on.

Quiet moved into the room. The kind of quiet that visited funeral parlors and gravesites. She shoved back against the chair slats. No pine boxes or black veils for her. Not if she had any say in the matter. Death would remain slumbering in its cold, dark crypt.

Her vision adjusted enough to the dim lighting that she could make out more of Gabe. A swath of cloth covered his eyes. Loops of rope bound his chest and secured his hands behind his back. Anger twisted inside her. Sloan might think he had the upper hand, but he had never met a tornado like her.

She laced her tone with venom. "Nate Sloan, you disgust me. You have no conscience, no morals. You think nothing of abusing others for your own gain."

Sloan turned his head. Moonlight spewed through the window and illuminated narrowed black eyes. Angry? Good. Hot heads clouded the senses. She wanted him to react without forethought.

"You're a filthy, selfish pig. That's what you are."

She tensed and readied herself for his attack. Once he moved closer, she would disable him with a kick to the groin. Sam had taught her how to protect herself against bullies.

He didn't take the bait. He remained rooted in place like a stubborn weed, staring at her as if she were a rock. She'd have to try another tactic.

"Do you really intend to drag us around the country, having Gabe do your bidding while the law is hot on your trail? You've only held us captive for one day and look how that ended up. Seems like a lot of trouble to me."

He waggled his pistol, the steel barrel glinting in the moonlight. "The only trouble is going to be yours and Sergeant Hunt's if you try anything stupid."

"Don't get your knickers in a twist, Sloan," Gabe said. "We're not going to try anything."

"See that you don't. If you want to stay alive, all you have to do is go along with my plans until I have a stake large enough to last the rest of my life."

It couldn't be that simple. Nothing in life was that simple. "And you'll release us after that?" she asked, even though the question sounded ridiculous to her own ears.

"Of course, I will. I'm a man of my word."

His word wasn't worth the breath he uttered it on. She opened her mouth to say as much but stopped. A faint sound trotted through the window. She cocked an ear. Was that horse hooves? Was her father returning?

Sloan must have heard the noise, too. He pasted himself against the side of the window and angled for a better view. A few seconds later, he let go a curse and scurried behind her. Clearly not the riders he expected.

He covered her mouth with his hand and rested the pistol barrel against her ear. "Keep still, pretty bird. And don't even think of yelling for help."

He smelled of sweat and stale tobacco. She held back a gagging retch. She needed to keep her wits and her dinner intact. This might be her only chance to save herself and Gabe.

She curled back her lips and opened her mouth as wide as she could. Sloan was going to discover this pretty bird had a very sharp beak. She snapped down on a finger, shoving her teeth into weathered flesh. Sloan yanked his hand away with a yelp. She ducked and leapt out of the chair. The door and freedom were only a few steps away…

Something smacked against the side of her face. She fell to the floor, ears ringing and head reeling. A salty tang filled her mouth. The evil Satan's spawn had drawn blood. It would be the last time he touched her.

She drew her leg under her and kicked out. Hard.

Her heel connected with bone and flesh. It gave way beneath her thrust. Sloan grunted and grabbed for his knee. He wobbled and stumbled back against the wall with a thud.

A rapid banging blasted from the other side of the room. She turned and caught sight of Gabe's chair rocking back and forth. It teetered on one leg and then toppled over. He crashed to the floor, his head smacking the boards with a loud thump. He went still, and her heart sank. Had he hurt himself? She had to get to him.

A quick glance confirmed Sloan remained propped against the wall, groaning and rubbing his knee. Disabled, but for how long she couldn't say. A booted foot would have been a more effective at disabling him than a bare one. She had to hurry.

She scrambled to her feet and rushed forward. There was a scraping noise, and then footfalls pounded after her. Her pulse galloped. She had to make it to Gabe before Sloan got to her. She lengthened her stride. Something swiped at her foot. She lost her balance, and the floor came up to meet her for the second time in as many minutes. She sprawled on her belly, gasping for breath. She was so close. Gabe's head rested a mere arm's length away.

A talon curled around her ankle and bit into her flesh. Her insides recoiled. No. No. No. Sloan would not regain control over her. Not this time.

She lunged forward and stretched as far as she could reach.

Her fingers met cloth.

She dug in and peeled off the blindfold. Tawny eyes blinked and met hers.

"Do it, Gabe," she hissed. "Stop him with your gift."

Chapter Fifteen

His pulse pounded. His mouth tasted like spoiled apples. His greatest fear had come to life. Either he used his gift and risked putting the woman he loved in danger…or back down and pray Sloan didn't do something irrational.

Unfortunately, the latter didn't seem likely. Sloan hoovered over Meg, pistol drawn, his expression dark and roaring for retaliation. She had gotten in a few good licks trying to escape from the thug. Thumps and Sloan's pained grunts had carried clear across the room. And if he had to guess, that gimpy knee he was favoring would be smarting for weeks.

"Leave her be, Sloan."

The thug ignored his warning and captured Meg by the waist. He hauled her to her feet and held her in front of him, gun barrel shoved to her temple. His eyes were black and empty as his soul.

"Don't try anything, Hunt. Or your little hellcat will be looking at the ugly side of the flowers."

Her perfectly coiffed hair was mussed. Her skirts were twisted and bunched around her thighs. A red streak of blood snaked from the corner of her mouth. His blood heated. Sloan would pay for mauling her.

"Last chance, Sloan. Let her go, or you'll be the one fertilizing the daisies."

Floorboards squawked beneath Sloan's shifting

stance. Antsy. Not a good sign. The man usually held himself with an iron fist. This lack of control could lead to deadly recklessness.

He kept his voice low and non-provoking even though his insides churned with a need to do something. "You know what I can do, Sloan. Give it up."

"I ain't giving up nothing. You're the one that's going to lose it all."

The pistol barrel sank lower and cradled a pink ear. A soft whimper cut across the short distance. Meg's pleading gaze drilled into him. He clenched his teeth around a curse. That was it. No more attempts at reasoning with a madman. He would let his gift do the talking.

He gathered energy in his head. His temples pulsed. Warmth swirled in his skull, rushing, building. He gave a push. Sloan's pistol tilted upward and away from Meg's head. A shot rang out. The bullet plowed into the ceiling, spewing splinters and dust.

Meg's scream set the hairs on his neck standing on end. His gut clenched. Had the bullet grazed her? He'd tried to make sure the barrel cleared her head but couldn't be certain it had.

She began twisting and turning, trying to wrench free of her captor. Fingers clawed at the thick arm trapping her waist. Not hurt then. Just mad as a wet hen.

In a movement so quick he barely caught it, she shoved a heel up and into Sloan's groin. The man grunted. She kicked again. Sloan buckled over. Damn. Whoever taught her to fight like that, thank you.

She bent over and twisted. Sloan's grip surrendered its hold. She stumbled away from him and dropped to her knees. Sloan wobbled but managed to lower his gun hand and level the pistol barrel at her head.

Oh, hell no. Gabe gave a hard push. Using the same tactic Meg had employed with her escape, he made the gun twist and jerk free of Sloan's grasp. He sent the weapon soaring skyward until it hovered overhead like an angel of death. But he wasn't like Sloan. He would always choose mercy over vengeance.

He pushed again. The pistol flipped over and plummeted downward. The butt end crashed against skull bone. Once, twice. Sloan slumped and crumbled to the floor. He lay there, motionless as a pile of manure but still breathing. Gabe grunted. Easiest nut he'd cracked in years.

He guided the pistol to the floor near his bound feet and then shut down the flow of energy. An ache throbbed in his skull where he'd struck the hard wood when the chair finally succumbed to his frantic rocking. He closed his eyes. The skirmish had taken more out of him than he imagined. He could sleep for a month of Sundays.

Footfalls clattered closer, and then warm hands began playing over his face, tapping, stroking, urging him to wakefulness. "Are you all right, Gabe? Speak to me."

He pried open his eyes and fell into a troubled blue gaze. She knelt beside him, her face pale and lined with worry wrinkles. He itched to soothe her fears, to kiss away her pain. All he could do was wriggle in his bindings.

"I'm fine. Just a little sore from being tied up so long."

"What did you say? Can you speak up? My ears are still ringing from having that gun go off beside my head."

He raised his voice. "I said, I'm fine. What about you? Your mouth is bleeding. Did Sloan do that?" Too bad it had only required two whacks to take the thug out. He deserved at least a dozen wallops.

She swiped at the blood with her sleeve. "It's nothing. I'd like to think I gave better than I got."

He smiled up at her. "You did, sweetheart. You did. Who taught you to fight like that? Sam?"

"Yes. He wanted me to be able to defend myself in the event I was trapped without a weapon." She shifted her reviving efforts to the rope confining him to the chair. "Let's get these bindings off of you."

He wagged his head. "You'll need a knife. Sloan tied them real tight. I haven't been able to loosen them one bit."

"Can't you use your…um…whatever it is you do with your mind and undo the knots?"

"I have to be able to set my eyes on whatever I want to move. With the knots tied behind my back, my talent is useless."

"Oh, that's unfortunate. Let me see what I can do with them." She grasped a loop of rope and pulled. The rope wouldn't budge. She swiveled around and set her feet on his arm, using them as leverage. She tugged harder, her face contorting with the effort. Still no movement. If she wasn't so serious, and the ropes weren't so damn tight, he would have laughed.

Fretful lines bunched her brow. "I can't get…these ropes are way too snug."

"It's all right, sweetheart. You tried. The soldiers will cut me free. It was them I heard riding down the street earlier, wasn't it?"

She relinquished her grasp with a sigh and sank back with her hands propped behind her. "I think so. Whatever Sloan saw outside the window spooked him."

"Probably the patrol returning earlier than he expected. Go and get them and the sheriff. They'll want to get Sloan behind bars before he comes to."

Her gaze raced to Sloan. More lines cratered her face. "I don't want to leave you. Not with him. What if he wakes up while I'm gone?"

"I'll be fine. Go on, now."

"But you must be uncomfortable lying on that cold floor. I can try to get the chair back to rights if you want."

"You'll only hurt yourself trying. I can manage like this for a little while longer. Believe me, I've endured worse and for much longer."

She stroked his face, her hands soft and loving. "You shouldn't have to endure anything. You went against what you knew could be dangerous and used your gift. For me. For us. That took an immense amount of bravery."

"Am I forgiven then for not using my gift on the train?"

She wound her finger around a tuft of hair and tugged, not hard enough to hurt, but enough to get his attention. "You are forgiven for not using your gift. As to keeping it hidden from me, that I won't tolerate. You must promise that there will be no more secrets between us. None. And to that end, you must let me make my own decisions regarding my well-being. I will not be dominated, by you or anyone else."

Most of that need to be her own woman came from a place where her father had put her. He wouldn't do that to her. He loved her too much for that. "I give you my word that I will not keep any secrets from you ever again. And I will not attempt to control or contain you. I will only offer advice which you can heed or not. It will be your decision."

She leaned over and pressed a brief kiss to his lips. "Good. I will hold you to those promises, Gabriel Michael."

More of those kisses would be nice, but such sweetness would have to wait. She needed to go for help before Sloan regained consciousness. And also before Tucker returned from the Golden Nugget with the Craven brothers. "Go, Meg. Get the sheriff and your father. We can talk more later."

As she gathered her feet to rise, footfalls scuffled outside the door. She froze, eyes going wide. "Who is that?" she whispered.

His pulse raced. He wriggled against his bindings. "I don't know. Sloan sent for more men. It could be them. Grab Sloan's gun. It's down by my feet."

She scooped up the pistol and swung around, putting herself between him and the danger at door. He opened his mouth to tell her to take cover behind him but clamped his lips shut. He'd just promised to let her make her own decisions. That needed to start now.

The latch jiggled. Meg thumbed back the hammer and aimed the barrel at the door. His heart swelled. Bravest damn woman he'd ever met.

"I wouldn't come in here if I were you," she called out. "I have a loaded pistol pointed at the door, and I won't hesitate to use it."

"Meggie?" a voice replied. "Is that you?"

He stiffened. He recognized that voice. He'd heard

it hundreds of times, mostly spoken in exasperation and disappointment.

She lowered the pistol and scrambled to her feet. "Yes, Father, it's me. You can come in. It's safe."

The door careened open, and General Myer raced into the room, followed by half a dozen soldiers, one of whom toted a lantern that spewed light into the darkened room. Gabe blinked against the abrupt brightness. Footfalls thumped closer. He tilted his head and met a fierce gaze. Just his luck to be hog-tied to a chair when his commander arrived.

"General Myer, sir," he said. "I would salute, but I'm kind of tied up at the moment."

Myer's expression didn't waver. He holstered his pistol and glanced at the unmoving man on the floor. "Is that the train robber Nate Sloan? We apprehended three men slinking about outside. One of them finally divulged who they were and what they were up to."

Gabe nodded. "That's him. He was holding us hostage while waiting for those other three you caught to arrive."

The general motioned to two of his troopers. "Collect that scum and haul him over to the jail. If he comes to and tries to escape, shoot him."

As the troopers rushed to carry out his orders, General Myer turned to Meg. Narrowed eyes softened. The harsh set to his lips faded. The man truly did care for his daughter.

"Are you all right, Meggie? Did that thug hurt you?"

"I'm fine, Father." She sank to the floor, set Sloan's gun beside her, and then pulled his head onto her lap. "But Gabe could use some help. I tried to untie the knots, but they are too tight."

His commander merely grunted and glanced over his shoulder. "Private Smith, come over here and cut Sergeant Hunt free. Bring that lantern with you so you can see what you're doing."

He knew Smith. Jackson kept a six-inch Bowie strapped in a sheath at his side. Said guns weren't as reliable as a blade for up-close fighting. Right now, all he needed was for the weapon to slice through hemp.

Meg's concerned gaze rolled over him. He gave her a reassuring smile. He couldn't wait to pull her into his arms and kiss away her worries. He glanced at his commander who watched over the proceedings like a hawk. Well, maybe later, in the privacy of a hotel room.

Private Smith set the lantern down and squatted beside him. He unsheathed his knife and sawed at the ropes. Within seconds, the bindings fell away. Gabe hauled in a deep, much-needed breath and then rolled to a sitting position. His hands and arms screamed with pain. He couldn't contain a grimace.

Meg's indrawn breath washed over him. "Oh, Gabe. Your wrists. They're bleeding."

"It's just a little rope burn. Nothing to worry about." He gathered his legs under him and stood. Meg rose as well and wrapped an arm around his waist as if to provide support. She was so thoughtful and caring. It was what he loved most about her.

General Myer stooped and picked up the pistol Meg has set on the floor. "Is this yours, Sergeant?"

"No, sir. It's Sloan's."

"Sloan's. Did you get the upper hand on him, Meggie? I'll bet he didn't expect to be overpowered by a proper little lady."

She pulled her bottom lip between her teeth. Blue eyes swam with indecision. He couldn't let her build a relationship with her father based on lies. It was time he came clean.

"No, sir, General Myer. Your daughter didn't overpower Sloan. I did."

"You did? How is that? You were tied up tighter than hog at slaughter."

Meg wagged her head. "Not now, Father. Gabe has been through a lot these past few hours. We should get him to a hotel where he can have those wrists cared for and rest. We can talk about what happened with Sloan later."

The general frowned. "Very well. But I want a thorough report in the morning, every last detail, no matter how inconsequential."

Gabe grunted under his breath. There was nothing inconsequential about the report he had to deliver.

Chapter Sixteen

Meg paced to the window and back. Her stomach roiled around the meager breakfast she'd managed to choke down. Sleep had been just as hard to nourish. She had worried all night over her father's response. Not his reaction at learning of their relationship. She would marry Gabe with or without her father's consent. No, she fretted because he might reject Gabe once he heard about his gift. His commander's approval meant a lot to him. Gabe would put on a strong front. Say it didn't matter. But she knew deep down, he would be devastated.

She plopped onto a chair with a grunt of exasperation. Why did life have to be so full of drama and discord? A sedate comedy would be nice once in a while. Sam had often employed theatrical antics to chase away her blues. He'd said, "Laughter is the best medicine." She could use a good laugh right now, or two, or three.

Sam. She rubbed her finger. His yellow remembrance string was gone. It had probably been stripped off during her struggle with Sloan. Before Gabe, she would have castigated herself for not being more careful. Now, she realized she didn't need any physical reminders of Sam. Those memories were all safely stored in her heart to be unshelved as needed. Gabe had also shown her that Sam's dismissal was not her fault. Sam had been exactly where he wanted to be, helping her. The ones to blame were those who were small of mind and big on bluster.

A knock echoed into the hotel room. Her pulse leapt. It was time. She drew in a calming breath, rose, and crossed to the door. She turned the knob and pulled open the door. Gabe stood on the other side, freshly barbered and looking resplendent in a crisply pressed uniform. He was composed and confident, and she couldn't have needed him more.

She dove into his arms. "Thank goodness it's you. I missed you so very much."

He wrapped his arms around her and pressed a kiss to the top of her head. "I missed you, too, sweetheart."

She rested her head on his chest. The even thump of his heart soothed her ragged nerves. With him by her side, everything would turn out just fine.

He unraveled his arms and gently pushed her away. "Let's get out of the doorway. Your father will be here shortly. I saw him downstairs speaking with the desk clerk."

She nodded and retreated into the hotel room. Gabe followed her inside, leaving the door open behind him. Wise of him. Her father was already upset with her reckless and improper behavior. Poking his sensibilities might make matters worse.

She stopped beside a set of table and chairs situated beneath a curtained window. A settee and a wing-back chair occupied the other side of the elegant sitting room. A connecting door led into an equally luxurious bedroom. Her father had insisted on securing her a suite in the best hotel in Guthrie. It was nice, but truly not necessary. She would much rather sleep in a bedroll under the stars with Gabe by her side.

He shucked off his hat and set it on an end table beside the wing-back chair. "How did your father come to be in Guthrie?"

"Quite by fate, so it seems. He said Mrs. Sommers and Private Dunn made it safely to Fort Dent about two days ago. They informed him what had transpired with the robbery and the theft of Orion…and of my headlong flight into the prairie."

One tawny eyebrow lifted. "It's a wonder we didn't hear his bellow all the way from the fort. His outrage can be quite deafening at times."

"He made his unhappiness quite plain when we met in the sheriff's office. No bellowing though, thank goodness. Once he learned of our plight, he gathered a patrol and began searching, starting with each of the train stops between Augusta and Mineral. His hope was to either find us stranded or learn of our whereabouts. He figured we were probably running low on funds, which of course, we were."

Frown lines creased his brow. "You look a little peaked. Did you not sleep well?"

She pointed to the bedroom door. "You would think having a plush, feather bed would send me straight to slumberland. But it didn't. Sleep was quite elusive. And you?"

"The same. I kept going over and over in my mind the best way to tell the general about us and about my ability. Every explanation I came up with sounded lame and ignoble."

The misery in his tone pierced her heart. She crossed to his side and rested a hand on his arm. "You don't have to tell father about your gift. We can fabricate some other tale that should satisfy him."

"No. I won't do that. Not to him, and not to you. It's best he knows about my gift now; else we'll be hiding it from him for the rest of our lives. Believe me, I know all about deceiving the people you care about. The duplicity will eat you from the inside out."

"We'll do whatever you think is best. It's your secret to tell. You know the general better than I."

He patted her hand resting on his arm. "I suspect the news of my gift won't upset him half as much as our unsanctioned relationship."

She curled her fingers around his, holding onto him. She would never let him go. "I don't care if he won't give us his blessing. I'm going to be your wife, one way or another."

Tender eyes caressed her. "You'll care. He's your father. You love him despite the years of separation."

"What will we do, then?"

"Leave it to me. I have a plan of how to reveal my gift to him."

A thought surfaced. "I hope this plan does not include any spilled wine." She titled her head and gave him a pointed look. "That was your doing in the Fred Harvey dining hall, wasn't it? Mr. Peyton didn't knock over his wine glass. You did."

"Why would I do such a thing?" He tried to look innocent but failed. Wretchedly. Twinkling eyes and a smug smile gave him away.

She shook her head. "Why indeed, you rogue."

"You applauded the calamity. Admit it."

"Perhaps."

The clearing of a throat bounced into the room. Her pulse skipped. She had heard that disapproving sound many times at Meadowdale Farms. Her father and Alma were definitely cut from the same cloth.

She slipped her hand out of Gabe's and turned. Her father filled the doorway, his stoic expression revealing little of his thoughts. She swallowed her last bit of moisture. "Good morning, Father. Please, come in and join us."

He grunted again and surged through the doorway. His authoritative presence spread through the sitting room like undiluted sunlight. Powerful and intimidating.

He tugged off his hat and tossed it beside Gabe's on the end table. "How was your night, Meggie?" His penetrating gaze took in the room. "You slept well, I trust."

Two men concerned for her sleeping habits. How lucky could a girl get? "Well enough. Thank you for your generosity in providing this lovely suite for me. It's quite comfortable."

"It's the least I could do after all you've been through."

He didn't mention her recklessness had been the cause of all she had been through. He didn't have to. It showed in the downward cast of his mouth.

He nodded to Gabe. "Sergeant Hunt."

Gabe snapped a smart salute. "Good morning, General, sir."

"At ease, trooper." He crossed to the table and pulled out a chair. "Shall we sit? I asked the desk clerk to send up some tea and sweet biscuits, your favorite, Meggie, or so Alma said in her letters."

He had taken the time and interest to learn something about her. That was promising.

Gabe relaxed his stance and tucked his hands behind his back. "Before we sit, sir, I'd like to discuss an important matter to the both of us…your daughter."

The general cocked his head, his expression more curious than annoyed. "Very well. Proceed, Sergeant Hunt."

"As you probably surmised, I wasn't too keen on being assigned to collect your daughter. However, after being around her and discovering her profound kindness and fierce loyalty, I have come to care for her a great deal. I am not perfect. But she is. Just being around her makes me a better man. I love her, and I will do everything in my power to make her happy. I would like your permission to have her hand in marriage."

She held her breath, waiting. What was her father thinking behind those narrowed blue eyes?

His gaze shifted from Gabe to her. "Is this what you want, Meggie?"

She tucked her hand in the crook of Gabe's elbow. "I do, Father. Gabe is everything I have ever wanted in a husband. Loving. Steadfast. In my eyes, he *is* perfect. Please, give us your blessing."

"Hmmph. I suspect you would wed despite my approval…but I give it."

Her heart danced. One hurdle crossed. One left to navigate. A big one.

A rattling noise sounded in the doorway. She turned and found a man dressed in a black uniform standing in the opening and holding a serving tray. Sweet treats. Her favorites. But she doubted her stomach would welcome any food right now.

"Your tea and biscuits, General Myer," the servant said.

Her father motioned to the table. "Excellent. Come in and set the tray over here."

The man strode into the room and placed the tray on the table. He dipped a bow to the general. "Will there be anything else, sir?"

"That will be all," her father said. "Thank you."

Gabe trailed the man to the doorway and handed him a coin before closing the door. An awkward silence descended over the room.

She pointed to a chair. "Have a seat, Father. I will serve the tea."

Gabe rushed behind her and pulled a chair away from the table. "No. Let me do the serving, Meg."

She looked at him, confused. What was he up to? He gave her a wink, and realization dawned. He wanted to *serve* the tea. She smiled and settled on the chair, fluffing her skirts and giving him time to marshal his confidence.

Her father sank onto the other chair and crossed arms over his chest. His raised eyebrows said volumes, but he remained mute.

Gabe stood beside the table, hands hooked behind his back, his expression calm. He had this under control, despite the reluctance she knew he had to be feeling. She couldn't be prouder of him.

"You asked for a full report on how I overpowered Sloan even though I was, in your words, tied tighter than a hog at slaughter. Well, here it is."

Gabe grew silent, his gaze rooted on the tea service. A slight twitch in his jaw was the only sign of movement. After a few seconds, the teapot slowly lifted from the tray and hovered over the teacups. It tipped and tea poured from the spout and into each of the cups.

Even though she knew what to expect, gooseflesh still crawled over her skin. His gift was truly amazing. And powerful. It was no wonder Sloan had wanted him for his own.

Her father's expression went from mildly curious to full-out astonishment. He blinked and blinked again. His mouth yawed like a fish out of water. She'd wager it was the first time he had ever been truly shocked.

The teapot settled back onto the tray with nary a sound. Gabe dipped a nod. "Sugar? Milk, sir?"

"How the hell did you do that?" Her father shot to his feet and swiped a hand over and around the tray. He then ducked his head under the table.

"What are you looking for, Father?" she asked.

"Strings. Wire. Hooks. Something to explain what I just saw."

"What you saw is Gabe's gift. He can move objects with his mind. It's how he subdued Nate Sloan. He was able to wrench Sloan's gun away and knocked him on the head with it."

Her father straightened and peered at Gabe. Fuzzy gray eyebrows snapped together into one formidable line. "How long have you had this...gift?"

"Since childhood, sir."

"Why didn't you advise me of this ability when you joined the army? It would make a most imposing weapon against our enemies."

Gabe's chin lifted. "I keep my ability a secret for many reasons, one of which is to prevent others from forcing me to use it against my will. It's the reason Sloan kidnapped me. He saw me use my gift and decided it would be a valuable tool for his criminal endeavors."

"You know I wouldn't order you to use your power for wrongdoing."

"I know that, sir. The other reason I held back is because it can have uncontrollable and dangerous consequences. A woman was killed by a stray bullet when I used my gift to overtake an armed and very angry cardsharp."

Her father's eyes widened. Red crept into his face. "Yet you still employed this aberration on Sloan and put my daughter's life in jeopardy?"

His tone had gone from incredulous to enraged in the blink of an eye. Gabe's expression turned equally stormy. Her stomach churned. She had to diffuse the situation quickly, before either of them said something they would later regret.

She pushed to her feet, heart hammering against her ribs. "You have it all wrong, Father. Gabe didn't want to use his gift, but I begged him to. Sloan was becoming irrational and had to be subdued before he hurt one or both of us. I trusted Gabe to keep me safe."

Her father shook his head. "I don't know. This is just too bizarre. I'm not sure I want Meg around such an abnormality. I must rescind my approval of your request to marry my daughter until I can give the situation more thought. I need time to absorb what this means for Meg."

Anger overrode her disappointment. She hooked hands on her hips and gave him a pointed look. "Don't think too long over it, Father. Or you will miss yet another important event in your daughter's life."

235

Epilogue

The path opened onto a large clearing. In the middle sat a massive two-story farmhouse. She reined Orion to a stop and took in the sight. Inviting rockers and potted plants dotted the porch stretching across the front. Mullioned windows reflected the cheery sunlight. The wallboards were whitewashed, and the door painted a pleasing yellow. It looked like a white-robed angel with her arms thrown wide to embrace visitors.

"This is it. Welcome to Seaton House, Meg."

"Oh, my goodness. It's so warm and cheerful." She pointed to the porch. "And inviting. No wonder you love this place."

"I love it and everyone who lives here. They are my family, my friends. I wouldn't be the person I am today without them."

She gave him a tender smile. "Then I shall be certain to thank them for having a hand in making the most wonderful man in the world."

"Keep saying that and I might just believe it." He quieted and a pensive look crossed his face. He bobbed a nod. "Sally just told me everyone is around back."

"She told you. Like whispered in your head told you?" Gabe had mentioned his sister had a gift similar to his. Instead of moving objects with her mind, she could send mental messages to other people, akin to a one-way telegraph.

"Exactly." His brow bunched. "If being exposed to our strangeness all at once is going to be too much, I can ask everyone to curtail using their gifts. They will understand."

"No." She nudged Orion forward. "I want to meet your family as they are. No veils or false fronts. I have had enough of that to last me a lifetime."

His horse fell into step beside hers. "Did I ever tell you how much I love you, Meg Myer?"

She turned her head and met his loving gaze. "Only a thousand times."

"And I'll tell you a thousand times more. A million times more. No, make that an infinite number of times. Down here on earth and into the Hereafter."

"Do you have a connection with the Hereafter that tells you we will be together after death?"

"No, but I know someone who does. I'll introduce you to her. Nel is her name. She's married to Sergeant Reese. She can talk with the departed."

Her pulse tripped. Would Nel be able to relay a message from her mother? Oh, how wonderful that would be to hear from her after all these years. "Does Nel only talk with people she knows, or can she talk with strangers?"

He shrugged. "I don't know the exact details of how her gift works. Most times, the apparitions come to her unbidden, both people she knows and those she doesn't. They seem to hover around the living with whom they have a connection."

"That sounds fascinating. If Sam were here, Nel wouldn't get one minute of respite from his questions. Oh, that reminds me; I meant to tell you..." Giddiness surged inside her. "Father gave me a letter that came a few days before we were scheduled to arrive at Fort Dent. It was from Sam."

"That's wonderful. I know you were worried about him. What did he have to say?"

"He learned I was going to Fort Dent to live with my father and decided to let me know how he was faring. He wanted to put me at ease, so I wouldn't worry about him." A laugh bubbled up. "He knows me well."

Gabe nodded. "He's a good friend. I know you miss him. Maybe we can take a trip to visit with him. Where is he staying?

"In Louisville, Kentucky. He secured a position at Elmendorf Horse Farm. He says they raise thoroughbred racehorses. He has been placed in charge of a stallion named Salvator who has won numerous races."

"It sounds like Sam is doing well."

"He's happy, so that's all that matters." Despite their rocky start, she and Sam had found new lives full of love and happiness. She couldn't wish for a better outcome.

She reined Orion around the back side of the house. A short distance away, a long, linen-draped table laden with food sat beneath an enormous oak tree. Lots of food. And lots of people, nearly two dozen of them, young and old. Male and female. They all went about their tasks with enthusiasm, smiling and calling out to one another.

A boy about ten years of age broke away from the group and trotted toward them. Gabe reined his horse to a stop. "We can dismount here. Robbie will take care of the horses for us."

She halted Orion and unhooked her leg from the saddle pommel. Gabe dismounted and came around to help her down. He set her on the ground, hands lingering on her waist. Heat spread under her ribs. His touch was ever so magical. Just like Seaton House.

The boy approached and gathered the horses' reins. Orion dipped his head and nuzzled the child's chest. A broad smile creased a freckled face. She couldn't help but smile as well. Horses and children always warmed her heart.

Gabe clamped a hand on the boy's shoulder. "This is Robbie Edmunds. He is a wonder with animals. Robbie, this is Miss Myer."

Robbie doffed his hat. "Pleased to meet you, Miss Myer."

"You must call me Meg." She nodded and broadened her smile. "We'll soon be family, after all."

Robbie stroked Orion's muzzle. "Your horse Orion is happy to be here in the territories. He likes his new home at the army stable. Says he has made a lot of new friends."

She cocked her head to the side and studied the boy. Had Robbie fabricated the tale to make her worry less, or did he truly know how Orion felt? And how did he know the stallion's name?

Gabe laughed. "It's true, Meg. Robbie is gifted like me. He can hear the thoughts of animals and they can hear his. Orion is happy to be here."

What a wonderful gift to have. Robbie was truly blessed. She patted Orion's neck. "Tell him I'm happy that he's happy."

Robbie smiled and tugged on the reins. "He knows."

As the boy led the horses away, Gabe held out his arm, crooked at the elbow. "Ready to meet the rest of my family?"

Her pulse leapt. She liked people. Just not all at once, and not when she was the one on display. She rested her hand on his arm, grateful for the anchor. "Ready as I'll ever be."

"Don't worry. They will love you just as much as I do."

She hoped so. She wanted to be a part of anything and anyone who loved Gabe.

As they drew closer, dozens of pairs of eyes turned in their direction. Smiles and delighted nods greeted them. Her unease retreated. They knew nothing of her, and yet she was being welcomed with open arms.

A familiar cheery smile and an owlish gaze blinking behind wire-rimmed spectacles greeted her across the short distance. Mrs. Sommers had recovered nicely from her head wound and had regaled the entire fortress with a thorough account of the train robbery. No detail went untold, not even her unceremonious dumping onto the railcar floor.

Meg waved to her friend. It was reassuring to have someone from her side of the family at the event, even if they weren't blood kin. There were several men in uniform among the guests. Private Dunn stood near Mrs. Sommers with his arm in a sling. He too was recovering nicely from his gunshot. According to Gabe, it wouldn't be long before the doctor released him to return to his regular duties.

The other trooper standing with Dunn was Sergeant Reese, Nel's husband. She had met him once during a visit with the convalescing trooper. He was a nice fellow with twinkling green eyes and a wit to match. He had her and Private Dunn laughing at his amusing anecdotes.

A few feet from the group, another uniformed man stood with his back to her. He was shorter and stockier and had gray hair. Her breath hitched. No. It couldn't be. The man turned and familiar blue eyes took her in. She pulled to a stop, stomach roiling. Three days ago, her father had declined Gabe's invitation to attend this celebration. Was he here to cause trouble? If so, he could just climb on his high horse and be gone.

He left the gathering and steamed toward her and Gabe. His stoic expression gave little clue as to his intentions.

"Father. What are you doing here? I thought you had other commitments."

He stopped in front of her. "I am here because I want to be here. I wouldn't miss this important event in my daughter's life for anything."

"Does this mean what I think it means?"

"It does. I wholeheartedly give my blessing on your marriage." His cheeks dimpled with a smile wide as an ocean. He leaned in and gave her a kiss on the cheek. "I wish you all the happiness you deserve, Meggie."

Her heart soared. His love and acceptance were the best gifts he could ever give her. "Thank you, Father. That means a lot to me. To us."

He extended a hand to Gabe. "Welcome to my family, son. I see a lot of myself in you. The good parts, that is. I envision a great future ahead for you and Meggie."

Gabe's face radiated with joy. His smile matched

his commander's. He took the general's hand in his. "Thank you, sir. I promise to love and care for your daughter for the rest of our lives."

An older woman approached her face a beacon of warmth and acceptance. She stopped and held out her hands. "I am Mrs. Campbell, caretaker of Seaton House. Welcome to *our* family, Meg."

Meg reached out and found her hands clasped in a loving grasp. All around her, welcoming greetings rose. Her heart soared higher. "Thank you. Thank you all. This is the most perfect engagement party a girl could ask for."

Mrs. Campbell turned. "Mr. Hoggard, would you deliver the blessing so we can start our celebration?"

The crowd parted, and an older man stepped into the middle of the circle. He wore a tweed suit and cap. He had a kind expression. One that would not judge.

"God, our Father in Heaven…"

She closed her eyes, listening to the benediction. Love and warmth caressed her. She felt accepted. Connected. This was where she belonged.

A word about the author...

Donna Dalton lives in central Virginia with her husband, two sons, and grandson. An avid reader of historical romances, Donna uses the rich history of the "Old Dominion" State for her story settings.

You can visit her website at:

www.donndalton.net

or on Facebook at:

DonnaDaltonbooks

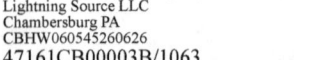